JODY FELDMAN

THE SEVENTH LEVEL

Greenwillow Books
An Imprint of HarperCollinsPublishers

The Seventh Level
Copyright © 2010 by Jody Feldman

The text of this book is set in Palatino.
Book design by Sylvie Le Floc'h

Library of Congress Cataloging-in-Publication Data
Feldman, Jody.
The seventh level / by Jody Feldman.
p. cm.
"Greenwillow Books."
Summary: Twelve-year-old Travis is invited to
become a member of The Legend, Lauer Middle
School's most exclusive secret society, but first
he must solve seven puzzles.
ISBN 978-0-06-195105-3 (trade bdg.) —
[1. Secret societies—Fiction. 2. Puzzles—Fiction.
3. Behavior—Fiction. 4. Middle schools—Fiction.
5. Schools—Fiction.] I. Title.
PZ7.F3357752Se 2010   [Fic]—dc22   2009021390

10 11 12 13 14 CG/RRDB 10 9 8 7 6 5 4 3 2 1
First Edition

 Greenwillow Books

For Jennie Dunham,
who insisted I tell this story first

CHAPTER
■ 1 ■

I'm free! I want to run through the halls and slide down the banisters, but every classroom still has kids and especially teachers, so that would be stupid.

Anyway, Senora Torres said, "Be quick, Travis." Or really, "*Rapido, Travisito.*" And she did let me out to fetch the once-alive, now-stuffed blowfish from my locker even though I was supposed to bring it, first thing, to class.

I go downstairs, slurp from the drinking fountain, peek into Matti's science room and make a face at her without the teacher seeing, then I turn the corner to go back upstairs.

When I open my locker to get my blowfish, it's not the only weird thing there. Balanced on my emergency 3 Musketeers bar, there's a big blue envelope. Not normal blue, but shine-under-the-surface blue like my favorite Hot Wheels car ever.

TRAVIS RAINES is marked with black Sharpie in perfect teacher handwriting. Then stamped all over are the words, FOR YOUR EYES ONLY.

My eyes are the only ones in the hall, unless that clock has eyes. And it shows I've been out of class just three minutes. How often's a kid at his locker without eyes around?

Besides, some reverse burglar broke into my locker, and that's not right. Unless . . .

No. Impossible. But it's blue! And a kid can hope, right?

The envelope's held shut by a string that winds around two dime-sized plastic circles, one on the flap and the other on the main envelope part. I unwind and unwind and I want to rip the thing, but the envelope's sort of plasticky itself and not rip-able.

Inside's a sheet of paper with some math problems. Well, woo-hoo. What's so top secret about that? Paper clipped to it is another piece of paper with a lot of writing.

I want to read it, but that wouldn't be so *rapido*. I can start, though.

Travis Raines,

You have been chosen for this game of sorts. Trust us.

You will want to do

"OH MY G—" I clamp my hand over my mouth and shove the envelope back into my locker just before Mr. Gunner sticks his head out the door.

"Aren't you supposed to be in class, Mr. Raines?"

"I'm getting something for Senora Torres."

"Then be quick and quiet."

"Yes, sir." But how can I be quick and quiet when this might be an invitation from The Legend? I need to jump. And whoop. And run around. I especially need to read on, but Mr. Gunner stands with his shoulder in the door frame.

I leave the envelope and math sheet in my locker, but the letter's coming with me. I fold it the long way again and again until it's skinny enough to hide under the band that runs around the cap I'm wearing for Lauer Middle School's first-ever cap day.

The cap, though, isn't mine. It's Kip's antique, team-signed 2000 Super Bowl Champion St. Louis Rams cap. He thought it'd be safer with me than in his stinky gym locker.

I take the cap off my head and—

Mr. Gunner spins around. "You have three seconds to get back to class."

I shove the paper into my pocket and slam my locker closed. With the blowfish inside. I fumble with the combination, open it, grab the blowfish, and race back without Senora Torres yelling that I've been gone too long.

Everyone crowds around her desk and oohs and aahs over the real Ecuadorian gold nugget in place of the blowfish's eye. That's why it's here. Yesterday, we learned *oro* means gold, and I mentioned the hunk in my blowfish.

Senora Torres wants me to tell the class about it. I want to go back to my desk and read that paper, so I skip the part about liking blowfish so much. How they start small but know how to grow bigger, especially when they're in trouble. "My dad felt—"

"Ah-ah, *Travisito. En español*," Senora Torres says, but how can a seventh-grade kid who's in Spanish class only forty-seven minutes on weekdays for less than eight months talk about this *en español*? It took me more than twelve years to learn this many words in English.

"*Mi padre* felt bad because he was in Ecuador on my tenth birthday, so he brought this back as an extra *regalo*."

"*Si viaja mucho?*" asks Senora Torres. "Does he travel a lot?"

I nod. "He speaks *cinco* languages so his company sends him all over," I say really fast, ditching more attempts to do this in Spanish. "He's in Japan now, but it's not my birthday, so when he comes back he'll stick with tradition and bring me an interesting fact."

"Eh-dweeb! Eh-dweeb!" The cough-word comes from Randall, the oaf who almost killed Jackie Muggs in fourth grade. Literally. Jackie's parents sent him to another school after that. No one knows why Randall was allowed back here. We just try to stay away from him.

"Eh-loser!" Randall's stinky breath coughs again as I duck out of the crowd and slip back to my desk.

Marco, a lesser oaf, laughs, but only so Randall won't try to kill him, too.

I take off Kip's cap and put it next to mine. With the two caps as shields, maybe I can read more of the paper.

I unfold it, hoping I'm not delusional and the mystery paper really is from The Legend. No one knows anything about the group except the members always use blue, they put on amazing school events, and they make you pass a test before they let you in. I cover the first two lines of the paper with Kip's cap and start with the numbered section.

#1 Everything in this envelope and in each one to come is to remain strictly private. "For Your Eyes Only" means

I whip my head to the right and shove the paper onto my lap. "What?" I say to Randall, who's now hovering over me. Can't let an oaf like him see my note. I refold it and jam it into the lining of one of the caps, staring at him the whole time. Once it's safely inside, I glance down to see which cap I used. Kip's. I can't switch it now. Not with Randall looking at my desk. And no matter how many times I keep raising my hand, Senora Torres won't let me put my blowfish back into my locker so I can also make the switch and read that paper.

Ringle-ringle-ringle! Ringle-ringle-ringle! The bell! Finally!

"*Hasta mañana!*" says Senora Torres. She heads right out the door.

I head right to her desk, grab my blowfish, turn back around and—

There's only one cap! "Where's Kip's—"

"No!"

It's sailing out the window.

CHAPTER
■2■

Randall's hand jerks back inside. I run to throttle the big smirk I expect he'll flash me, but he sticks his head out the window like Marco and some other kids do.

I squirt through, ready to see Kip's cap with my letter lying two stories below for anyone to steal, except . . .

Except everyone's looking up.

"You oaf!" I yell, not caring if he tries to kill me to.

"I wanted to look at it by the window," Randall says. "See if the signatures were real or if someone stamped them on. Then—"

"They're real." I jut my head out, but I can't believe

what I'm seeing is real. My stomach lurches like a milk shake maker.

Kip's cap is somehow stuck to the brick wall between the roof of the school and the second floor where we are. At least I don't see my paper snake on the ground below.

I could kill Kip. Why didn't he listen to me and keep his cap on the fake head in his bedroom? Why didn't I jam that paper inside mine? Why did I leave both caps alone?

I keep looking up, praying for the wind to blow the cap off, but the wind today couldn't blow a dead leaf off the point of a pyramid.

"What's going on?" Kip's voice.

I close my eyes and bring my head back inside. Time to tell him about half this mess.

"Randall threw your cap out the window," I say.

Kip's freckles pop out on his face. His lip color disappears, too.

"Did not," says Randall.

"Sure," says Marco.

Randall glares him quiet. Marco's lucky that's all Randall did.

Right now their war doesn't matter. Other stuff does. It matters I might have lost my invitation to become part of The Legend. It matters Kip trusted me to keep his cap safe, and I didn't.

Idea. "Someone get the whiteboard markers."

I kneel on the bookcase below the windowsill. With one hand plastered to the inside of the window, I maneuver my head and shoulders outside—the only advantage of being puny.

"Kip, hold my legs. Tight."

Randall's stronger, but I wouldn't trust him with an ant's life.

"It's too dangerous, Travis," says Kip, latching his beanstalk fingers onto my ankles anyway. "The wind'll blow the cap down."

"Yeah," I say, inching out the window. "The wind'll pick up in the middle of the night, blow it away, and some oaf will have himself a priceless cap that belongs to you. Just hold on."

His fingers grip tighter and his weight presses down.

"Marker."

Someone hands me one. I hurl it up. Right direction but not close enough to the bricks.

"Another." It hits the wall too low.

"Another." I arc it an inch short.

"Another."

"Let me try," says the oaf responsible for this.

"No way."

Someone hands me the eraser. I heave it up, up, up, and over the cap.

"Another."

"There is no other," says Randall.

"Then get one."

"What about baseball practice?" Randall says.

"Leave," I say. "Someone else! Get me something to throw."

"No," Kip says, pulling my ankles back in. "It'll fall on its own. Maybe after practice."

I come back in, and Randall's gone. "He really left? That oaf!"

"What a wimp," says Marco. "If you wanna get him back . . ." He double pounds his chest.

I thought all oafs stuck together. I almost give him a smile, but Kip tugs me toward the door. "C'mon, Travis. I don't want Coach to yell at us."

Coach always yells at me. Everyone yells at me. Or at least gives me those looks.

"Get it over with, Kip. Yell at me for once." We speed to the locker room.

"Not your fault," he says. "We'll get it."

Why's he so confident? He should be furious even if he's never been mad at me no matter how much I mess up. He'll just flash his cockeyed smile that means he's worried. Usually about me.

We change lightning fast and barge out.

Matti's racing toward us, her black hair bouncing behind her. In the next ten seconds she'll have it bound like a ball in a hair band until it unravels into a messy ponytail a minute later. It has since she was two. But it never stops her from playing better than most boys. That's why Coach lets her stay on the team instead of sending her to girls' softball.

"You're late," she says, then turns and sprints toward the door.

I run past her then outside toward the cap side of the school. She catches up and matches my stride. Kip pulls in two steps after we stop. I kick the whiteboard markers and eraser against the wall so I can fetch them later. Then I point up.

Her eyes open wide. "Yours?" she asks Kip.

He nods.

"How'd it—"

"Randall," I say. "I turned my back for three seconds and—"

"Don't beat yourself up," says Kip. "You didn't throw it out."

"But it was on my watch," I say. "I'm gonna get it."

Matti shifts her eyes back and forth. "How?"

I sigh. "Don't know."

We hear shouts from the field. No one says anything. We race to practice, but I'm not thinking about bats and balls. I'm thinking about Matti's question. How can we rescue Kip's cap and my paper inside it?

CHAPTER
∎3∎

After practice, we head to the cap side of the school. Yes! It's still there. I tug Matti's sleeve and stop by the loading dock. She tugs Kip, and we let the rest of our team pass.

I'm not sure what the cap's stuck on. Probably a nail that holds up Legend Event banners. If I knew who was in The Legend, I could ask how they get the banners up and down, and I wouldn't have to do what I'm about to.

I let the loading dock corner scratch my shoulder. When the other sweaty bodies are far enough ahead, I point my chin up. "I'm going up there. I'm gonna get it."

Matti smiles. Big.

Kip smiles. Cockeyed. "It's not worth it."

I look at him like he's nuts. "Not worth it? Your dad'll kill you."

"He won't either."

"I know," I say. "But you'd do this for me."

Kip shakes his head.

"Okay," I say. "Maybe you wouldn't do *this* for me, but how many times have you bailed me out? First, when the oaf knocked over my easel and you missed recess to help me clean—"

"That was kindergarten, Travis."

"Then my lunch on top of the cubbies. The oaf again."

"Travis," says Kip. "First grade. I was taller."

"Fine. Second gr—"

"Stop. My fault I brought the cap to school," Kip says. "You can't take this risk for me."

It's not only for you. It might be for me and The Legend. "What risk?" I say instead.

"One, there's you killing yourself. And two, if you're not lucky enough to kill yourself, there's Principal Wilkins."

"He's not the one I worry about. You know that." I turn to Matti. "Please?"

"Oh no," she says. "I'm not stupid enough to try and distract her. It's like she has her radar gun aimed at you, Trav."

"Which is a good thing," says Kip. "Otherwise, you would've pulled the fire alarm."

"There was fire in the room. And smoke."

"It was a makeup science lab with a teacher," says Matti, adjusting the band holding her hair. "There was supposed to be fire, and you weren't supposed to be at school."

I try not to turn red. "Actually," I say to Matti, "I don't need you to distract her." I point to the assistant principal's parking spot. "See? Her truck's gone. There's only . . . what? Like three cars left. I need you in case she comes back. Just be my lookout."

Matti's ponytail whips around. She nudges Kip. Looks at me.

I stare back at her. "You're the only person for the job. We all know she lo-oves you."

"I can't help it if Mrs. Pinchon likes me, so don't imply I'm a suck-up."

I shake my head. "I didn't call you a suck-up. But if the name fits . . ."

Kip takes a step back to dodge the words that could start flying, but now's the wrong time to mix it up. Even if we do it in fun. "Forget it," I say.

Matti looks up, way up. "I don't think you should do it."

"What?" I don't need her permission, but she seems to know what I can get away with.

"I don't think *you* should do it," she says. "Randall should clean up his own mess."

Sure. Randall would do that, and I would walk through fire. Barefoot. Doused with gasoline. "One problem. Do you see him here to fix this?" I ask. "Just watch out in case Mrs. Pinchon comes back, okay?"

"No way," she says. "If you're doing it, I'm watching."

Kip grabs on to Matti's arm. "He's not doing it."

They lock eyes again like they have for about a year. Like they're gonna run off and kiss. It makes my neck prickle.

Kip lets her go and turns to me. "I once heard that there are one million ways to mess up a murder, and if you can think of fifty, you're a genius."

"I'm not murdering anyone."

"Maybe your own self," Kip says.

I don't wait for Kip to tell me the rest of the bad things that might happen. "Just stand underneath so I know exactly where to go."

I creep into the building even though Mrs. Pinchon is gone. It's like she knows me better than I know myself, and

it wasn't only the fire alarm last week. It started when she was introduced during the first-day-of-school assembly this year. I had to go to the bathroom and was wriggling in my bleacher seat, and I swear she burned her radar eyes into my bladder and made me sit still till the end. Right then I knew I was in trouble, and I will be for all of middle school unless she retires real soon. Someone said she already retired but came back when our old assistant principal's wife got a new job in Toledo and they needed to find someone fast.

So even though I am allowed in the school, I duck under the windows to the main office. Then I flash down the side hall to Mr. McKenzie's custodian closet and borrow a strong piece of rope. I go upstairs to the teachers' lounge, where teachers only lounge during school. Not after, I hope, or some school adult'll haul me by the ear to lifetime detention.

I knock. No answer. I slip in, around the vending machines, through the roof access.

Cool. Way up here, it's like I'm tall. I tower over Kip and Matti and now the whole baseball team. Except Randall. He's conveniently absent.

"Travis Raines! Are you nuts?" Marco yells.

"Maybe. But I'm not stupid." I hold up the rope so they see it, then I tie it to my waist and hook the other end to a not-too-rusty pipe that juts from the roof.

"Trav!" Kip yells. "Maybe Mr. McKenzie has a ladder in his closet. Even I'd climb that."

"Not tall enough," I call back. "Where do you think I got the rope?"

"What about a ladder and a stick? Or a long fishing pole?"

"Yeah. Like anyone brings a fishing pole to school."

"You brought a fish," says Marco.

I laugh and tug at the rope tied to the pipe. That should hold. Unless the pipe breaks. But I'll only need the rope if I slip, and I won't. I'll be quick, I'll go home and have a snack, Kip'll have his cap, and I'll have my paper.

I lie flat on my belly, my head peering over the edge to line my body with the cap that, for sure, is stuck on one of The Legend's nails. Seven more nails sit in the same row on a big area of brick wall about three feet below me.

Idea. Kip might've been right about the fishing pole. If I tie this rope to a rock or a stapler or something to weigh it down and lean over the roof and knock the cap . . .

Nah. Too much trouble. I'd have to untie myself, come down, raid a teacher's desk to find something heavy, get caught, and be accused of stealing. This'll be faster.

I wave below. Then I pivot on my stomach and stick my feet over the shallow ledge that runs around the edge. With my torso still on the roof, I lower my legs more and more until I'm an upside-down L. I turn my head a little. "How close am I?"

"You can't do it," says Kip. "You can't get close enough."

"Yeah, he can!" yells Matti. "Move about three inches to your left, then you have two or three feet to go."

Two or three feet? Great. I'm four foot eight, and two feet something of my spindly legs are already dangling. I was hoping I'd need to hang down only to my armpits. Now it's gonna take work to hoist myself back up.

I wish Kip had my arm strength. He's about eighty-three feet taller than I am and would've been able to kick off the cap by now. Maybe Matti would, too, but I don't like to remember that her legs have suddenly grown higher than my waist.

I take a deep breath and ease down, brick by brick, my toes catching on mortar indents just enough to control my descent.

"One more inch," Matti calls from below.

Good thing. The concrete ledge is starting to sink into the insides of my elbows and at my first knuckles, where I know my fingertips are turning white.

My right toe reaches for another brick, but something stops it. Something hard and sturdy. Something I can rest my weight on for a minute.

"That's it!" Matti calls. "Kick it off."

I will in a sec. . . . "Ahh!" I will now. My footrest bends down. My fingers grab tighter.

Someone screams below. Then come the cheers. I did it! I—

What did I get myself into? The blood is pounding in my temples. I can taste my own sweat. I don't want to go down with the cap and become tonight's news.

Pretend its gym class, Trav. Do one more chin-up, and you'll break the school record and—and—and I can't swing my legs forward to pull myself up. There's a wall in front of me.

Don't panic, Trav. You have your emergency rope. It'll hold. It'll hold until a firefighter . . .

No firefighters. I can't be caught. Not again. Not by anyone, especially Her.

I try to jam my baseball cleats between the bricks. Too thick. Why'd I have to wear these? Why couldn't I have worn, what? Flip-flops? To baseball practice? If only. Yeah.

"Trav," calls Kip. "You're scaring me. Go back up."

"I will. Just look out below."

I scooch my shoes off my heels and listen for two thuds, relieved no one yells because the cleats have hit them on the head. I also don't hear anything except running feet. Maybe they're all racing to congratulate me. Which they can't do if I splat like that pumpkin we—

No. Concentrate. Fingers. Knees. Feet. I latch my toes on to the mortar between the bricks, and in two seconds I'm back on the roof, looking at the angry lines in my arms.

And into the angry face of Mrs. Pinchon, assistant principal in charge of discipline.

CHAPTER
■4■

"I thought . . ." I don't bother to finish my sentence.

"You thought what?" Mrs. Pinchon looms over me, talking with that deep Southern drawl. "I was gone?"

I try not to nod, but my chin seesaws up and down.

"Things aren't always as they appear, Mr. Raines. Remember that." Mrs. Pinchon kicks the roof pipe I tied my rope to. Either she has high heels of steel or the rusted pipe wouldn't have saved my underwear from flying off the roof. From its new busted-open, lying-down position, the pipe releases the rope to Mrs. Pinchon's hands with me at the other end like a guilty dog. Or her prisoner.

We walk through the roof access door, and I gulp my voice quiet. It wants to tell Mrs. Pinchon to take her own advice. Things aren't always as they appear. What she thought was me dangling from the roof was really a tree shadow, so if everything's good, I'm outta here. With me on a leash, though, I'd be stupid if I didn't keep quiet and follow her to her office. I'd be just as stupid if I untied the rope. But if it accidentally unties itself . . .

My fingers act on their own and play with the knot. By the time we're on the first floor, Mrs. Pinchon is walking a leash attached to nothing. I'm still following.

She glances back, then shoots me a look.

I shrug. "Maybe I'm not a good knot tie-er."

Did I see a splinter of a smile on her face?

Wishful thinking, with all the things she could do to me. At least she can't string me on a flagpole through my earlobe. I don't think my parents want my ear pierced.

She can't expel me either. They didn't expel the eighth grader who brought drugs to school the first time. He got suspended.

Can't Mrs. Pinchon understand? Today I was trying to fix things, but she probably can't understand more than rules in a rule book.

After she closes her office door behind me, she doesn't

haul out the book. She swivels and rocks in her body-swallowing chair.

I know it swallows bodies because last spring I barely scrambled out before the old assistant principal caught me. I try to stop grinning.

"What're you so happy about, Travis?"

"Your chair?"

"Is that a question or a statement?" Her eyes burn so hard into mine, I'm afraid she'll turn my green ones brown like hers. I'm also afraid to tell her I don't know how to answer her question.

"My chair makes you happy?" she asks, saving me from admitting it.

"It looks comfortable."

"Then try it." She stands and sweeps her arm toward it like a model showing prizes on the old game shows my mom watches. But Mrs. Pinchon's not close to model pretty.

I can't stop staring at her eyebrows. They're like a pair of sideways question marks: reddish, sort of drawn on, and half-hidden by the red bangs that look permanently plastered to her forehead. I never noticed her eyebrows before, probably because I don't usually make eye contact with assistant principals in charge of discipline. I have no choice today, now that I'm sinking into this chair. It was more fun last time when I was sneaking a seat.

"Do you still like my chair?" she says, moving to the other side of her desk.

This is no time to disagree with anything. I nod.

"Good." A dangerous smile creeps onto her face. "I want you to sit there and walk in my shoes, so to speak."

I bite my lip to keep from laughing.

"What's so funny?"

Does this lady know everything? "I'm sorry, Mrs. Pinchon. I was picturing me walking in your shoes. Your high heels."

She turns away from me, I'm hoping, to hide a smile. "Do you think this is the proper time for such thoughts? Shouldn't you be thinking about your little stunt?"

"It's hard," I say. "My brain keeps flooding with what you're gonna do to me."

"Which is why I have you sitting in my chair," she says. "I want you to be me. What punishment would you give yourself?"

Me? All I can think about is grabbing my passport from my dad's top dresser drawer and fleeing to Micronesia. "Can't we look in the rule book to see what's appropriate?"

"That's the problem," she says. "The rule book doesn't cover suicide missions."

"I wasn't gonna kill myself."

"You could have, and schools don't like when that happens." Is that a joke? Should I laugh? Nah. Better listen. "So, Mr. Raines. Appropriate punishment?"

I should get the worst over with. Maybe not the worst, which would be banning me from The Legend, tied with banning me from soccer next fall. Okay, the next worst. "I wouldn't suspend me," I say. "I wasn't mean, I didn't hurt anyone, and it's not good for a kid to stay home from school. You don't learn anything, you get bored, then you get into more trouble. Especially a twelve-year-old kid like me with both parents working and only my dog at home."

"I agree," she says. "I don't think suspension befits your actions. Other ideas?"

I watch myself in the mirror-ball necklace she always wears. It sways back and forth, back and forth, trying to hypnotize me. "Detention," I say in my new hypnotic state. I can handle smelly detention after school and still catch the end of baseball practice.

Mrs. Pinchon nods. "Detention. Settled. For how long?"

Am I deciding my own punishment? Cool. How long? She looks too serious for one day. This is Tuesday. "The rest of the week?"

"Fine," she says with another sweep of the arm that sends me to the wooden chair on the other side of her desk.

"Are you gonna call my mom now?"

She sits, rocks back, her chin resting on her fingertips. "No. You get the pleasure of telling your parents all the gory details." She starts typing at her computer.

Why can't she call and get this over with? How do I tell my mom what happened without freaking her out? How do I get that paper from Kip's cap without telling him about it? I wait forever with nothing to do but stare at my own face staring back at me through the ADA PINCHON letters on her gold nameplate.

Finally Mrs. Pinchon triggers the printer. "This will be for your parents to sign," she says. "And detention for the rest of the week? That's appropriate. But . . ."

I hate "but." "But" can make you scrape dried-up gum from under the desks or clean the gym lockers with—

"But I don't know if that's creative enough for your offense."

Huh? Will "but" have me tap dancing in detention?

Or wearing a fairy costume to gym class? "I don't know exactly what you mean."

"I mean," she says, "your actions don't fit any guidelines, so your punishment shouldn't either." She glances out the window. "Ah. Here comes Mr. McKenzie with my pickup and those cases of toilet paper the supply company forgot to deliver today."

My punishment involves the janitor and toilet paper?

Idea. "Can my punishment be to help in a safer way? Like helping Mr. McKenzie?"

She lets out a short laugh. "Why not, Travis? Go help Mr. McKenzie."

My lungs breathe easier.

"But also, according to this letter, you're to be standing in front of your house tomorrow morning at seven sharp looking for my pickup. I'm your bus, your bicycle, and your legs the rest of this week. You'll spend your detention here in my office, seven o'clock until school starts, then after school until I take you home. Around five-thirty. Something, thankfully, you weren't aware of before you climbed onto the roof."

CHAPTER
■5■

My mom makes me stand outside at ten to seven. In the morning. Before the sun's all the way up, before my stomach's ready for breakfast, and probably before Randall's out of bed. He should be standing here, the oaf. Not here but outside his house. It's his fault I got in trouble and couldn't get my For Your Eyes Only paper from Kip last night.

At exactly seven o'clock, I'd guess, Mrs. Pinchon's truck rounds the corner to our street.

I try to smile and bounce to the driveway, hoping a good attitude will let me out of jail to find Kip this morning, but my smile and bounce are still tucked under my covers.

"Good morning, Mr. Raines," she says.

"Morning." I swing open the navy blue door and hand her the Travis-has-been-bad letter my mom signed. It gives Mrs. Pinchon permission to rule my entire life through Friday.

"Don't look so glum. Not everyone has his own personal chauffeur."

I give her a piece of a smile because she's right about that. If only I could choose the time and I could choose the chauffeur. It sure as shirt dirt wouldn't be her and it wouldn't be now and it wouldn't be in a pickup.

She chatters about moving here from Texas and loving St. Louis and doesn't once bring up my little stunt, as my mom also called it. At least I don't think she does. It's hard to listen when your toes feel like eighty-three pickles crammed into a ten-pickle jar.

I had to wear my old shoes because I never found my baseball cleats yesterday and Mrs. Pinchon didn't let me get my stuff from my gym locker. I rode my bike home in sock shreds after I helped Mr. McKenzie lug ten more-than-half-my-height cases of toilet paper into the school. So I'm also trying not to flex my arms, which will be sore. Until the Fourth of July.

We pull up to the building and there, hanging on the

bricks where Kip's cap hung yesterday, are two huge banners. The first is a new one, Legend blue, painted with floating money. The second one has been around for years: a blue triangle and square, interwoven. The symbol of The Legend.

Normally I'd get run-in-circles excited, but I can see myself stuck in Mrs. Pinchon's office while every other kid is winning prizes or playing soccer all day or doing whatever The Legend dreamed up. Whoever they are. No one knows how The Legend members get picked or where they meet or how and when they hang the banners. No one knows how they've been able to keep everything secret for so many years. But everyone hopes for one thing: to be a member.

I point to the banner.

"Yes?" drawls Mrs. Pinchon.

"What's the Event?" I say, chickening out from asking the real question.

"You'll have to wait and see."

"Will I get to see?" That's the question.

She doesn't answer for what seems like hours. Instead she pulls into her parking space. "I can't punish myself or any teacher by making one of us stay behind with you."

I follow Mrs. Pinchon down the noiseless hall into her

lightless office. This dark, her chair looks like a grizzly, and her coat rack with her spare jacket and hat looks like a burglar.

She sets her briefcase on the bear's lap, gives her *I Love Lucy* lunch box to the burglar, and puts her purse in her desk drawer. Then she turns on the lights. She points to a small table and chair on the same wall as the door. "I took the liberty of having Mr. McKenzie deliver this here, seeing as you'll be my guest this week."

No video games? I'd better not joke. Instead I drop my backpack next to a card that's white at the top and stapled to a strip that's puke yellow on the bottom. I hand it out to her.

"Oh, right," she says. "I need you to read this and sign."

The white part says I'm her slave for life. Or not. Just that I recognize I've been a bad boy, and if I continue to do dangerous stuff, I may not get all the privileges other kids get and blah, blah, blah in little print on the white part. I sign the puke yellow strip.

She files it in her top desk drawer, swivels in her chair, and turns on her computer.

I sit at the little table and try to figure out what The Legend's up to.

Legend Events can be anything. In October they set up a rubber duckie pond in the school swimming pool and donated the ducks to some group—Bath-Deprived Kids of America, we joked. That was nice and all, but the best part was everyone got to fish out a duck and win the prize printed underneath. Oh, and when Zach Giatta fell in, then about six other people jumped in and the teachers only got fake mad at us. Legend Events are always free passes to go nuts, but just a little. It's like we know not to cross some line into evil or they'll take The Legend away from us, and no one wants it to end.

Most of the duck pond prizes were one dollar bills or free homework passes. Kip won a pizza party in the teachers' lounge for him and seven of his friends. This eighth grader won Principal for a Day, the grand prize. Mine was one of seven to skip class and deliver pencils and notebooks and other supplies to a school where kids can't afford them. We got to ride in that cool Lookout Transportation Services bus with its tinted windows and four rounded couches for seats. Then we got ice cream on the way back. That was the best prize.

Or not. The best is being in The Legend. Those kids decide everything good that goes on in this school. The duck pond was a small Event. Others are so big that sometimes a magazine or newspaper or TV station runs a story about them. The Legend people are always photographed from the back, wearing their royal blue robes with hoods and . . .

Royal blue? Shine-under-the-surface blue? The Legend!

I can't believe it yet. Lots of things are blue. Besides, if I was getting into The Legend yesterday, my roof incident probably killed it by today. Some giant Legend Head could've taken the blue envelope out of my locker as easily as he put it in. Which he couldn't have done if I already had it. But Mrs. Pinchon's eyes were watching me until I left last night.

I pray it's still there, but I can't ask to go and see now. We just got here.

"Ahh."

Mrs. Pinchon looks at me. "Something wrong, Travis?"

Everything. "Two things," I say, remembering something else. "I need to tell Coach Ford why I won't be at baseball practice this week. . . ."

Mrs. Pinchon holds up a finger, gets on the phone, and tells Coach to come to the office. "And the other thing?"

"It's probably not what you want to hear, Mrs.

Pinchon," I say as politely as I know how, "but exactly what am I supposed to do this morning?"

"Your homework, read a book. . . ."

"Great. Now you sound like my mom."

She smiles. Big. "And what did you say to your mom?"

"That I already did my homework, and I don't know anything worth reading."

She exhales. Loudly. "While I take care of that," she says, "why don't you take care of these." She opens a drawer, pulls out my baseball shoes, then leaves.

There's a rule against wearing cleats to class, so I stuff them into my backpack, wishing she'd send me to my gym locker to change into shoes that fit. For now I'm stuck here with nothing to do besides explore her office.

The photos on her wall are of kids at this school. Not family. Did she ever get married? Or did people joke and call her Mrs. Pinchon since she was born much longer than forty years ago. One diploma is almost that old. Another is dated twelve years later, and the third is from less than two years ago. When I'm her age, you won't catch me going back to school.

I sit on my hands in her chair so I won't touch the papers fanned on her desk. I look, though, to see if anything's about The Legend or me. Yellow invoice for the toilet paper. Blue sheet about school clubs. White one with . . . Ooh . . . can't see. I reach and—

Ka-link-ink-ink!

Keys. Why can't Mrs. Pinchon carry jangle keys like Coach Ford does?

I go to the door to meet him.

"Travis," he says, holding the *s* in my name. "I don't think I want to see you here."

I tell him the story.

"And what's our motto?"

I look near his elbow. "Play smart," I say. "Sometimes I forget when I'm off the field."

"Do I need to bench you?"

I look him straight in the eye. "No, Coach. No."

He stares at me like he's trying to decide.

I'd be more nervous if this were soccer, the best game in the world because it doesn't care how short you are. Still, I don't know if I could sit there and watch the others swing and stretch and run. "I didn't mean to get into trouble. I was trying to do something good. I promise."

Coach Ford stops staring. "Remember when we were going back to school after last week's game? Remember what you told me?"

I shake my head.

"You explained how you apply lessons you've learned on the field to your life."

"I said that?"

"Well, I think that's what you meant when you said something about loving sports because they let you make up for your mistakes the next time the ball comes your way."

That's what I was doing with the cap. Why can't any adult see that? "Yeah," I say. "I was trying, but I guess I wasn't smart enough."

He leans against the door. "You're still playing soccer next fall?"

Oh no. Where's this going?

"Yeah. I mean, yes, sir. I mean I'd be playing soccer right now if we had spring soccer. You know that."

Mrs. Pinchon strides in and plops a pile of books onto my table. "Hello, Coach." She looks at me then looks back at Coach.

"I was just about to tell him," Coach says.

This can't be good.

"Remember our last game this year?"

"We lost in the playoffs. Overtime."

He nods. "Remember how your effort led us to a last-second tie to take it to overtime?"

I can remember every detail. Dribbling the ball, passing to Matti, getting it back, evading the defender, and kicking it over the goalie's head with about ten seconds left in the game. The taste of my sweat. The smell of the grass. The roar of my team. But I just nod.

"And I'm sure you remember it's tradition for the season's most valuable player to become co-captain the next year."

So this is where it's going. I nod again. I can't talk. I can only see Randall's big oafy face, grinning, taking my place.

"Don't look so glum, Mr. Raines," says Mrs. Pinchon. "You haven't lost that. Yet."

Coach puts a hand on my shoulder. "We'll watch you the rest of this year, Raines. You think you can stay out of trouble and play smart in every respect?"

"I will. I promise."

Coach shakes his head.

"I promise I will really, really, really try."

He almost smiles. "If you can accomplish that, you might get to wear that captain C next year." Coach turns, goes halfway out the door, then reels back around. "Stop messing up."

I won't mess up. I won't mess up. I won't mess up. How will I not mess up?

I sit and knock my head against the table until I remember Mrs. Pinchon's here.

I look up and wait for her to hammer home Coach's point, but she points to the books she brought in. "For you. A mini library. Something to do."

Whoopie. I look at the spines. Read it. Saw the movie. Saw the movie. Didn't want to see the movie. Heard of it. Never heard of it. Never heard of it. Saw the movie. Read it. Saw the movie. Never heard of it.

These could be the best books in the world, but I can only think about soccer and The Legend and how everyone'll be watching me forever. Like her.

Mrs. Pinchon turns, her mirror pendant reflecting my nose then the door then my nose then . . . "What is it, Mr. Raines?"

"About yesterday? I'm really, really sorry," I say.

"I'm sure you are." She shifts in her chair like this scene is over and we're about to start a new chapter of the book I've landed us in. Problem is I don't want to read this book. Don't want to read any book. I want to read that mystery paper.

She twirls her pendant between her thumb and fingers, and I watch my face spin.

"Why don't you go ahead and read, Travis. Or do

some extra homework, or twiddle your thumbs and stare into space. Or answer this," she says. "How did you know about the roof access in the teachers' lounge?"

"I was there for The Legend pizza party in October."

She shakes her head. "The access door is around the back behind a closed door."

I shrug. "It's a good idea to know where all the fire exits are, and every school's required to have an escape map, so it's easy to find."

"You've studied the fire plan?"

"You can test me," I say. "From here the closest exit is to the right and out the front door. Unless that's where the fire is. Then you'd either—"

Mrs. Pinchon raises her hand to stop me, obviously not interested in fire maps. She just rummages through her drawer, then holds up the whiteboard markers and eraser from yesterday. "It's almost seven thirty," she says. "Return these to the proper classroom. Then use the bathroom and visit your locker if you need. Be back before the buses start arriving. Five minutes."

I break free from Mrs. Pinchon's dungeon and start to run down the deserted halls to Senora Torres's room. But that's not a smart way to start this probation thing they've got going for me. So I walk and return the markers. Then I pick up speed and run-walk to my locker. I can't help it. I can't wait to see if my secret envelope's still there.

It is! So's the math sheet. I jump up and down eighty-three times, race to the locker room, change into my normal shoes, then run up one hall, down the next and—

Footsteps and chatter echo toward me. The buses. I speed back toward Mrs. Pinchon's office. Back with a shiny blue envelope buzzing in my fingers.

CHAPTER
■6■

I hide the envelope underneath my shirt before I go into the office, but Mrs. Pinchon doesn't even look up. That's an old principals' trick. They try to be invisible so they can jump at you when you forget they're there.

I won't forget. I move the envelope into my backpack, slip out the math sheet, then stand *Gulliver's Travels*, one of the thickest books, on the table as a cover. I stick my face into page eight but stare down at the math. The numbers start looking like hieroglyphics. Actually, hieroglyphics would be more fun to look at right now. I could pretend the 8 is a shield and the 1 is a sword and the 6 is some sort of chariot. And that would mean—

Dernck. Dernck. Dernck.

I jump with the knock on Mrs. Pinchon's door glass. Cover the math sheet with the book.

Kip? He's nuts to be here. She'll blast him for ever associating with me, but Mrs. Pinchon's smiling and motioning him in.

He walks sorta crooked, like he woke up with a stiff neck, but that's his way of not looking at me. I can't blame him for trying to avoid trouble himself.

"Excuse me, Mrs. Pinchon?" Kip sways like his feet are stuck in cement. Still, the guy's got guts. "Travis left a homework paper with me yesterday and couldn't get it last night." He holds up the paper snake. I snuck-called and told him it was there, and private.

Mrs. Pinchon takes it. "Is this your handiwork, Travis?"

"Yes, Mrs. Pinchon."

"You're a good friend, Kip." Mrs. Pinchon smiles at him then turns to me with a not-as-pleasant face, like it's saying, "When will you let him rub off on you?" I want to suggest that Kip stick around to teach me to be good, but that might totally vaporize me.

Instead I mouth *thank you* and give Kip a thumbs-up as he walks out the door, where Matti's waiting for him.

"Show's over, Travis," says Mrs. Pinchon. "Back to work."

"No problem." I unfold and unfold and unfold, then flatten the paper out.

"Nice way to treat your homework," she says.

I wish I could do something right. I want to explain that I don't need to turn this in. I especially want to say it's Randall's fault, but it'd sound like I'm making excuses, so I apologize, and she goes back to her computer, which is an excellent thing because not knowing what's on this paper might kill me if I have to wait any longer.

Travis Raines,
You have been chosen for this game of sorts. Trust us.
You will want to do what we ask of you. These are the
rules.
#1 Everything in this envelope and in each one to come is
to remain strictly private. "For Your Eyes Only" means
exactly that. When you receive each new envelope, hide
it if others are around. Wait until the coast is clear. Our
eyes are everywhere.

#2 Every envelope contains instructions toward your journey to our Seventh Level. Follow what they say and you will receive further instructions.

#3 Solve every puzzle and perform its ensuing task quickly. Time is of the essence.

#4 Solve every puzzle and perform its ensuing task alone. If you are stumped, you may ask questions that sound as if you are looking for homework help. You may NOT show anyone your puzzles. You may NOT let anyone solve a puzzle for you.

#5 Your parents understand the secret nature of your actions and the limited role they are allowed to play.

#6 Remember, when opportunity closes a window, it often opens a door.

#7 Only after you solve every puzzle and perform every task will you be privilege to our secrets and rewards . . . assuming you follow every rule.

This has to be The Legend! It has to be! I gulp down my energy and study the math sheet.

. . . 1035, 828, 621, 414, ___ . . .

. . . 8, 16, ___, 64, 128 . . . - 51, 32, ___, 14, 25, 16, 17, 18 -. . . 4, 9, ___, 25, 36 . . .

Travis, it would behoove you to solve this puzzle within three days. When you do, bring a circle there.

Bring a circle where? What kind of circle? A Frisbee? A doughnut? Or just something I draw on paper?

And what does "behoove" mean? Be a horse with hooves? No. "Betray" doesn't mean to act like a tray. And I belong to stuff, but that doesn't mean I be long. I be short. I hide my laugh with a cough.

Mrs. Pinchon looks up.

I want to say the book is funny, but as far as I know, this part's about death.

Idea. "Mrs. Pinchon, sorry to bother you. But do you have a dictionary?"

She nods.

According to the dictionary, it'd be in my best interest to do whatever this says. Sounds like something a principal might say. To a kid who's been dangling from a roof. What if this isn't The Legend? What if this is from Mrs. Pinchon? A principal's practical joke. But the envelope was there before the roof. Still . . .

"Travis?" says Mrs. Pinchon.

"What?"

"You sighed. Do you need anything?"

I sighed? "I guess I'm not used to getting here so early."

She nods. "Go on, then. I doubt you have enough time to get into trouble with just a minute until the first bell."

"I could pull the fire alarm."

Her glare doesn't see the humor.

"Just kidding."

I think I see a little smile as I go out of her office.

All morning, the teachers stop every bit of talk about The Legend Event. At lunchtime Kip's leaning on the cafeteria door, waiting with a look that says any Legend talk will have to wait some more.

I shake my head. "Don't say it, Kip. I found one of your billion ways to mess up."

"I wasn't going to say anything." But his lips twitch like they're dying to say, "I told you so." He forces them back into place. "I owe you, Trav."

I poke my pen point into the doorframe. "No, you don't. I didn't go on the roof just for your cap. I needed the paper," I say, almost wishing Kip would ask about it.

"But if I hadn't brought that cap . . ."

I wave him off. "Consider it payback for kindergarten and first grade. I still owe you for second through sixth, then for something you'll probably help me with this year."

Matti rounds the corner. "Travis! You're alive! Unscarred!" She grabs my hand and quick studies it. "She didn't hang you by your fingernails in her torture chamber? Or stretch you on the rack?"

"Do I look any taller?"

She bounces once around me. "No rack. You're right. Sorry." She doesn't look sorry.

I start walking to our lunch table. "Sorry about what?"

"I probably could've made sure Mrs. Pinchon was gone before I watched your Spiderman impression."

"That's what you're sorry about?" asks Kip.

"What should I be sorry about?"

Kip shakes his head. "For encouraging him. Travis doesn't need encouragement."

"I know that." Matti bounds around toward Kip. "I've also known him since birth, and there's no stopping him when he gets that look in his eye. You should know that by now."

They keep walking to our usual lunch table, even when kids stop me to say they're glad I didn't kill myself. Still others call out to me, and I try not to strut. Mrs. Pinchon and Coach Ford would not like this attention.

I get to my seat, and the other five look at me like I've risen from the dead.

"Yes, I'm alive, thank you very much." I open my lunch bag. "Anyone want to guess what The Legend Event is?"

"Travis!" says Matti. "Tell us already. Last night? This morning? Details. Now."

I give them a play-by-play of what went on after they bolted like rabbits.

I look at Kip. Amazing. He's taken only two bites of his first peanut butter and Bacos sandwich. He puts it down and puts on his sorry face. "No baseball for the rest of the week?"

"Not your fault, Kip." I look two tables away from us. Randall's shoving a cupcake into his face like he had no part in this. "He's the one who should apologize."

"The oaf." Kip takes a big bite of his sandwich.

"So, what'd your mom do?" says Matti. "Call your dad in Japan? Scream? What?"

"Worse. She freaked out that I could've splatted. It didn't matter that I was standing in front of her with all my blood inside my body," I say. "Then she went into this thing, how if I stop watching TV shows where the hero jumps from the tenth-story window into a Dumpster and walks away with nothing a shower can't fix, then maybe I'd remember I wasn't immortal, and I'd use my brain instead of letting TV put ideas into my head."

"Sounds like your mom," Matti says.

"Sounds like every mom," says Katie, the only other girl besides Matti who'd be good enough to play on the boys' soccer team if they'd let them. "What's your punishment this time?"

"I'm her total slave for two weekends. Plus I'm grounded from life for two weeks. No TV, no computer, no video games, and maybe no soccer camp."

"No soccer camp?" Kip sounds almost as panicked as I did when my mom hit me over the head with that.

"What's with you?" says Matti. "Even if Travis doesn't go, I'll still be there."

That's what worries me. Matti and Kip have been talking more lately and nudging each other, and I get this vision of them becoming boyfriend and girlfriend. I shake that thought and describe the part about me needing to be good forever or until school's out, whichever comes last, or I might as well throw myself into a volcano.

So while I tell them how my mom threatened that I could be weeding the garden for the entire summer, I stab my sandwich with a pretzel stick, trying to hit a Swiss cheese hole. I hit cheese. I pull out the pretzel and lick the end from the sandwich. At least I got mustard. But nothing tastes good now. I push my sandwich aside.

"You're not going to eat that?" Kip says, finishing his second sandwich.

I give it to him. My stomach's too loaded with blowing my chance for soccer camp and soccer captain and with two and a half more hours of solitary confinement just this afternoon.

It's also crammed with the secret of the envelope.

CHAPTER
▪7▪

Just two classes left today and still no Legend Event. When I get to Mrs. Bloom's science room, I walk straight to her. "Is there gonna be a Legend thing or not?"

She smiles. "The Legend doesn't make a habit of telling us teacher types much."

"Yeah. Right." I point to the non-shiny blue envelope on the lab table in front of her.

She turns it over so I can see what it says on the other side. "'Open only when instructed.'"

"I haven't been instructed yet," she says. "Believe it or not, Legend information comes on a need-to-know basis. Most of us don't even know who's in the group."

She gives me a small push toward my table. "Sit, Travis. Be patient."

Be patient? I hate that especially when it's my only option, but I can't afford to get in trouble again. I sit.

Mrs. Bloom's room is probably the most interesting in the school, with lab tables, microscopes, Bunsen burners, ecosystem displays, a static electricity maker, a rainbow tube, the periodic table of elements, Whiskers the live rabbit, dead taxidermist-stuffed animals, and the Toxic Closet—the one that equals instant expulsion if anyone breaks in. It's even locked with some thick, circle-stamped metal bar.

It's way past time for class to start, but Mrs. Bloom's just sitting there, thumbing through our textbook. Either she totally spaced out or she—

The intercom crackles. "Faculty? Please open your envelopes."

She does. In slow motion. "'Please bring your class to the cafeteria,'" she finally reads. Then she leads us out the door.

I wonder how they'll pack every kid at Lauer into the cafeteria without suspending half of us from the ceiling. But then a bunch of classes veer toward the gym.

We stop at the cafeteria doors, which have been

transformed into archways of canned food. When did they do that? How? And who? Was anyone missing from class? Great. I didn't pay attention.

"Hey, Natalie!" She always pays attention. I weave around a few kids to get to her. "Anyone missing from your classes this afternoon?"

"I don't think so. Why?"

"Legend people? Someone had to set all this up."

"Drat!" She looks around.

"What?"

"I always thought Zoe was in it, but she was in class the whole time. So was Amos."

I'm glad I'm not the only one who obsesses over things like that.

This guy, Mick, is standing right next to me. "I helped do it. Me and the janitors and about ten other people in my gym class. And believe me, none of us are in The Legend."

They lead us in, and the cafeteria is empty except for twenty clear-glass booths and three long tables spaced around the room. They make us sit on the floor, which also means on the grease of eighty-three million squashed french fries, but who cares? It's The Legend.

Principal Wilkins goes through his welcome-and-behave speech. If he'd move right to the interesting part, he wouldn't need to tell us to behave. No one's paying attention, but then Mr. McKenzie rolls a huge TV to the middle of the floor.

It gets quiet until we hear screams coming all the way from the gym. So we get noisy, too. Principal Wilkins gives up and hits a button on the remote.

A huge green dollar bill appears on the screen. Then music plays, and some guy's singing about money. "Money, money, money, money. Mo-ney!" The dollar bill starts fading in the background, and the guy . . .

"Ahh!" It's Chase Maclin!

No mistaking his messy black hair, black T-shirt, gold guitar, and trademark tiger chain.

We're all shocked it's Chase Maclin, but no one should be. He graduated from Lauer Middle and Lauer High School, and he's back in town sometimes. Rumor has it he has a recording studio—

"Hello, Lauer Middle School!" he says from the screen.

Screams peak.

He signals us to quiet down. I guess international rock stars know how kids'll react because it's not like he sees us.

"I'll keep this short," he says, "because you have only till the end of school today to collect money for the food bank."

I probably groan the loudest. The Legend cannot turn boring on me. Not now.

Chase zooms so close to the camera, his face gets all distorted. "Stop complaining."

We laugh.

"Most of you aren't hungry."

"I am!" I yell, but I'm not the only one.

"Who said that?"

It's like Chase knows us.

"But seriously, Lauer." He backs away from the camera. "People go hungry, really hungry, every day of the year. You guys who collected seven thousand cans before Thanksgiving, even you have forgotten that food pantry shelves empty out. Today it's your mission to fill them up."

We stay quiet.

"And that's where the fun comes in." Chase motions for us—or the camera—to follow him. "You didn't think we'd forget the fun?" He shakes his head. "You gotta have faith, man." He closes himself inside a glass booth like the ones here. "Watch this." Suddenly he disappears behind clouds of money blowing around.

Then we see his hand catching some. And more and more. Soon the money stops blowing, and Chase comes out with handfuls of dollars.

"You'll each have thirty seconds to catch as much as you can. Half the money you grab will go to the food bank. And if you want to keep the other half . . ."

Chase grins, waits for a few seconds to let the cheers die down, and taps his watch. "But if you turn in all your money, you might win prizes that are worth more than the few bucks you'll keep. Your choice. See ya!" He walks off the screen.

Principal Wilkins steps in and tries to tell us which classes are assigned to which money booths, but he gives up.

Kip and I stand together—apparently Matti's class went to the gym—and we study people trying to catch the bills. It doesn't look as easy as Chase made it seem. Maybe he practiced or he had more money in his booth. We decide to forget the money that falls to the ground because it blows back up right away. We'll concentrate on the bills flying between our stomachs and eyes.

Kip and I mimic the guy in the booth, trying to snatch money out of the air, but I stop to rub my arms. "I couldn't play ball today even if I wanted to."

"Because," Kip says, "if you're trying to get ready for a

game, you probably shouldn't go hanging off buildings."

Natalie and Marco and some other people turn and laugh.

"Here's more advice," Marco says. "Next time make a Legend person do it. Or Randall."

I'm getting to like this guy.

"Hey, Randall!" Marco calls him over. "Travis has sore arms from yesterday."

"So?" says Randall.

Marco rolls his eyes. "Just wanna give you credit, big guy."

I don't care if Marco's trying to suck up to him. I won't give Randall any credit for my pain. "It wasn't the roof," I say. "It was the toilet paper." By the time I finish telling them the story, they probably think I carried eight hundred cases of toilet paper to the storeroom plus eighty more upstairs to that pipe room near the teachers' lounge.

Most of the way through the story, Kip steps into the booth. He's grabbing everything.

"How great is this?" I say.

"It's cool," says Marco, "but why does The Legend get the glory when anyone can rent a money machine?"

"Still," I say, "what other school gets to do what we do?"

Kip's buzzer goes off, and he points to me with two fistfuls of dollars. "Your turn."

Mr. Gunner reminds me I can't touch any money on the ground until the wind blows and the green light flashes. And I need to freeze when I hear the buzzer and see the red light or lose my turn and everything I've caught. He opens the door. It might be my imagination, but I think he's watching me harder than he watched anyone else.

Wind! Money! Green! Go!

I ignore the pain and grab air. Concentrate. Got one! Another! Gonna lose them if I open my hands too much. Another! Stuff all three into my pockets. Grab. Stuff. Grab. Grab. Stuff. More. More.

Buzz!

I bend a little backward and catch a fluttering-down dollar on my chest.

Mr. Gunner opens the door.

"Can I keep this one, too?"

He gives me a look.

"I'm donating every dollar. I promise."

"We both are," says Kip, who waited for me.

Mr. Gunner plucks the bill off my chest and motions for me to step out. "I can't punish such flexibility." He hands me the dollar.

Kip and I head to the tables. We turn in everything—we each caught eighteen dollars—and I ask who got the most so far.

"Over there. He got twenty-five." The teacher points to Randall. Figures.

We fill out our entry forms and stick them into the prize-drawing box that shows what we can win: pizza party, random school supplies, double lunch period, and playlist composer for before-school music. Then, at the bottom:

GRAND PRIZE: BOX OF MYSTERY ITEMS,
ALL AUTOGRAPHED BY CHASE MACLIN.
VALUE: AT LEAST $700.
TO QUALIFY FOR THIS ADDITIONAL PRIZE,
BRING IN 5 CANS OF FOOD BY MONDAY.

Kip nods his head and just says, "Cool," in typical Kipness.

Me? I'm jumping on his back. "More than cool! Awesome! What do you think's in there? What's worth at least seven hundred dollars?"

Kips shrugs, but I'm still bouncing. Not only could I

win, but I don't have to haul five cans of food all the way here on my bicycle. I have a ride in the morning.

Now I just need a way to survive the rest of detention and figure out where I'm supposed to take that mathsheet circle.

CHAPTER
∎8∎

After school I'm back in my dungeon and itching to pull out my math sheet, but I'm not alone. But the way Mrs. Pinchon's hitting her keyboard, she wouldn't notice the difference between mystery math, homework math, and fireworks.

I take the chance.

$$\ldots 1035, 828, 621, 414, \underline{} \ldots$$

$$\ldots 8, 16, \underline{}, 64, 128 \ldots -51, 32, \underline{}, 14, 25, 16, 17, 18 - \ldots 4, 9, \underline{}, 25, 36 \ldots$$

The problem at the very left? In preschool, I thought

I was brilliant when my mom taught me one plus one is two and two plus two is four. I got all the way to 128 plus 128, which I thought was the highest anyone could add until she told me about 256 plus 256.

I write 32 in the blank.

Back to the top. All the numbers decrease. Minus 207, minus 207, and please. If you're gonna give me a test, give me a real test. Okay? No lame word problems either. I write in 207.

I look at the clock. If Travis has four math problems and solves the first two in three minutes, how long will it take him to finish them all?

Six minutes? *Bing, bing, bing!* Give that boy a prize!

At this rate I'll be done by three fifteen with only social studies homework left. Time to waste time. I slip down, flop my neck over the chair back, stick out my legs, and feel like the slidey part of a playground slide. My stomach bubbles. I poke it near my belly button, and it speaks to me.

Why'd I let Kip eat my sandwich? It would taste amazing now. Cardboard would taste amazing now. And no way she'll let me out to grab my emergency 3 Musketeers bar.

I poke my stomach again. This time it yells.

"Travis?" says Mrs. Pinchon.

I sit up. "Sorry."

"That's okay." She smiles, a real smile. "I should've thought about feeding you. We have vending machines in the teachers' lounge, but you know that."

I start to give her one of my best fake grins, but any principal who can joke with me deserves a real one.

"So, what's your poison?" she says.

"My poison?"

She gives a laugh. "No worries, Travis. It's simply a figure of speech. What would you like to eat?"

"I know," I say. "My grandma used to say that."

"Your grandma, huh? And what did you tell her?"

"Cookies."

"We have cookies," she says. "What's your favorite? Oatmeal? Chocolate chip?"

"Either's fine," I say. "The machine won't have my favorite anyway. Moon cookies."

Mrs. Pinchon looks at me like I spoke in Martian. "Moon Pies, you mean? Closest we have are chocolate-covered Oreos."

"No, I mean moon cookies, which look like moons because they're round and white and have poppy seed craters. My mom and I have been trying to make them the right way since my grandma died, but we haven't figured out the recipe yet."

"Sorry," she says like she really means it. "No moon cookies in the machine." She starts around her desk, toward the paper.

I throw my backpack over it then rummage around to see if I can come up with any money. "How much is stuff in the machine?"

"Don't worry about it," she says, heading toward the door. "Principals have power over school vending machines."

I don't know if she's kidding or not, but my stomach's relieved. Can't even find a penny.

"So chocolate chips? Oreos?"

"No," I say. "Only moon cookies would taste good to my tongue right now. So, is there something cheesy in there?" Like my cheese sandwich conveniently digesting in Kip's stomach.

"I'll be back."

I wish she'd find moon cookies. My mom made a batch last night but accidentally sprinkled the tops with salt instead of sugar so we threw them all out and—

And why am I just sitting here? Even if Mrs. Pinchon jogs all the way upstairs, down two halls, gets me something to eat and rushes back, she'll be gone for at least three minutes.

Maybe her computer has something about The Legend or Chase's mystery box or even why Randall gets away with everything, including knocking me into the bushes after practice last week. I could unload for three hours about everything he's done, starting with Kip's cap, but I'm not a snitch.

Neither's her computer. Whatever's on-screen is disguised behind some jungle screen she must've clicked on before she got up. I'd minimize it, but there's no telling if I could click it back in time. Good-bye, spying. Back to mystery math.

I look at the next problem.

51, 32, ___, 14, 25, 16, 17, 18

The numbers go down, then up, then down, then up. I write in the differences.

$$-19 \quad +11 \quad -9 \quad +1 \quad +1$$

51, 32, ___, 14, 25, 16, 17, 18

No pattern. No hint of a clue of a pattern except random nines and ones. No way to add or subtract or multiply or divide to get the next number. Forget this one. Next.

$$\ldots 4, 9, \underline{\hphantom{00}}, 25, 36 \ldots$$

At least these numbers don't seesaw.

The office door swings open, and Mrs. Pinchon puts a bag of cheddar Goldfish and a carton of orange juice on my table. I'd rather it be a can of orange soda, but I don't say that. "Sort of an orange theme, huh?" I say. " Thanks."

She nods, all businesslike, then she pounds away at her keyboard, frowning.

What'd I do? I thought we were making progress. I don't want to cause a backslide, so I try to open the Goldfish without making noise. Silent crunching is just as hopeless, but if I chew when she types, the sounds blend together.

I keep eating and sipping, and the orange energy clicks my brain into gear. *4, 9, ___, 25, 36* is obvious now.

Two times two is four, three times three is nine, four times four is sixteen, which I write in the space before the five-squared and the six-squared.

So, one more to go and I'm done. Or am I?

There has to be something else here, or I won't know where to take the circle and get the further instructions they promised in the rules.

I stare at Mrs. Pinchon's back. Maybe I give the circle to her. Okay, Mrs. Pinchon. I'll solve that last problem, give you a circle, and everyone'll break-dance. "Heh-heh."

"Mr. Raines?"

"Sorry. I got a funny picture in my mind, and my voice burst."

"I could use something funny about now. Why don't you share?"

That I'm picturing you on the floor, twirling on your back with your shoes getting caught in your skirt? "It's not that funny."

"You mean I wouldn't think it funny."

"I'll just go back to my math now."

"Suit yourself."

51, 32, ___, 14, 25, 16, 17, 18

This problem is different than the others. It has seven numbers and one fill-in-the-blank. The others have four numbers and those three-dot whatchacallits. What do they mean?

"Mrs. Pinchon?" I wait for her to look up. "What do you call those three dots that sometimes come at the end of a sentence?"

"Ellipsis?"

"That's it. May I please borrow your dictionary again?"

"Keep it on the table through Friday," she says, then heads to the door. "Be right back."

I should break-dance, but I find *ellipsis*, which is a symbol for "and so on." Okay. So in the easy problems, numbers come before and after what's shown, but the numbers in the impossible problem are the only ones allowed. What do they have in common?

Nothing. I go back to my slide position and hold the paper way above my face. Am I going bonkers? Is too much blood rushing to my eyes? I see letters shining through.

I turn the sheet over. Either someone's dyslexic or in kindergarten because, on the flip side, I see two backward *R*s and one backward *L*. A number sign, too. I turn the paper back, hold it toward the light, and the number sign shines through, over the first answer blank. The letters appear under the other three answer spaces. R L R.

I'm so close to figuring this out, my brain starts to tingle.

51, 32, ___, 14, 25, 16, 17, 18. I know what I'm missing. All the numbers are here except nine and zero. Is that a clue? Is the mystery number 90? No. Too random. The other sequences have patterns.

Ooh. So does this one. Five-ONE. Three-TWO. Something-THREE maybe? One-FOUR. Two-FIVE. One-SIX. One-SEVEN. One-EIGHT.

All right! But what's the pattern to the first digit of each number? Five, three, something, one, two, one, one, one. No pattern.

Maybe the answer will fly into my brain if I write what I have so far.

#

207

<u>32</u>   ___   <u>16</u>

R   L   R

Where have I seen something like this? Something set up with the R L R. What do the letters stand for?

R. Raines. Roar. Ransom. Ruler. River. Ripper. Rip. Rip. Rip. Wanna rip the paper. That'd get me somewhere.

Yeah, right. Right. Right? Right-left-right. I look at the original puzzle again. Why didn't I notice those before? Dashes. I add them in.

#
207
<u>32</u> – __ – <u>16</u>
R   L   R

I know this! A locker combination! Locker 207. 32 right. Something left. 16 right.

Hoo-hah! If the middle number is something-THREE, and if it's a school lock, it can only be three, thirteen, twenty-three, or thirty-three. I can spin that lock open in a flash.

That tingle spreads up and down my legs. I need to run, run to locker 207, and see if my Further Instructions are there.

First, though, I need to escape this dungeon. Legally.

CHAPTER

▪9▪

Mrs. Pinchon is now banging on the computer keys like she needs to pulverize them, not the ideal time to ask if I can search for locker 207. But if I tell her an almost-truth . . .

I wait for a pause in her keyboard attack. "Excuse me. Mrs. Pinchon?"

She turns enough so I see one of her question mark eyebrows go up.

"May I go-to-a-locker?" I sort of slur together. "And maybe to the bathroom?"

The brow raises higher, toward the clock on the wall. She nods.

My guess is I have five minutes before she sends her search dogs. I count ten steps from her office then race to the sixth-grade hall, where the locker numbers are lower. 419, 374, 313, 245. Then the hall turns toward the gym and cafeteria. Go.

Locker 1 to my left, 184 to my right. Where are 185 to 244? Only sixty lockers. Has to be in a small hall. Small hall. Library hall. I round the corner, full speed. Skid to locker 207. Lift up the lock. Spin—

Thum-runkle!

Trash can. Eyes! Mr. McKenzie.

"Travis Raines!" He and his broom are standing just outside the library door. "You're supposed to be in Mrs. P's office."

"I—I . . ." I-yi-yi. "Mrs. Pinchon. Yeah. Mrs. Pinchon let me out for a break."

"But not for breaking and entering, punishable under law, by both school and police. Should you be opening other people's lockers?" he says. "You're locker isn't here."

"This is a special case. Mrs. Pinchon knows. . . ." I look straight at him. "How'd you know my locker's not here?"

"All the ones in this hall are empty."

Now what? I glance at my paper. "Oh," I say. "Five oh seven, not two oh seven. See ya." I round the corner, duck into the boys' room, pee, flush, and wash. I have to know what's in that locker today. If I'm a few minutes over, I can tell Mrs. Pinchon I had bathroom problems and—

Problem! I forgot to bring a circle! I need to find one here. Why can't toilet paper come in circles? Or paper towels? I pull one from the dispenser, fold it in half and try to tear a perfect curve on the non-folded side. I open it up. Too bad The Legend didn't ask for a giant amoeba.

I need a circle. I could draw another one but no pen. And a water circle would dry before anyone finds it. A circle. A circle.

I am having bathroom problems, Mrs. Pinchon. The problem is there are no circles in the bathroom, not even the toilet seats. I reach into my pockets. Nothing. But I have a button on my shirt. Kids like me lose buttons all the time, Mom.

I start to yank one loose, but it feels like I'll rip a hole. I take my shirt off and bite the threads. I have a circle! Now I need to get to the locker without any eyes around.

In case Mr. McKenzie's still near, I fling open the bathroom door, thud some decoy steps in the wrong direction, then I turn and tiptoe the way I need to go. I crawl beneath the window to the library door, then crouch-walk to the locker.

I twirl the wheel a couple revolutions to clear the lock. Then I stop at 32, reverse and go to what? Three? Doubtful. All the numbers in the puzzle are two digits. Okay, 13. Stop. Right again to 16. Tug. Nothing. Next. Clear the lock. 32. 23. 16. Tug. Bingo!

The only thing in the locker is a blue envelope with my name and FOR YOUR EYES ONLY on the front. I replace it with the button then lift my shirt in back and wedge the large envelope part way into my pants. I close the locker, dash around the corner, then fast-walk back to Mrs. Pinchon's office and pause outside her door.

When I go in, I don't want to look like I'm hiding a secret. I try on a couple expressions, but they all feel weird. Instead I slip in like I'm trying not to bother an adult.

Mrs. Pinchon barely looks up, not even when I fidget to stop the envelope from clawing at my back. Not even when I ungrip my hold on the original puzzle sheet and smooth out the paper as much as I can. I write 23 in the last blank. But why is it twenty-three?

"You know why I don't like puzzles?" I mean to say to myself.

Mrs. Pinchon stops bashing her keyboard. "Why?"

"If you can't solve one, it creeps around your head like a slug until you find the answer."

She smiles. "Something I can help you with?"

I shake my head. "I need to figure this out myself."

"You'll have to do your figuring at home," she says. "I know it's ten minutes early, but I'm ready to leave."

Hoo-hah!

Even though Curry, my golden retriever, is the only one home when I get there, I lock my bedroom door before I free the envelope from my pants.

I unwind the string from the circles and spill out a weird, double-stacked coin. One side's the size of a double-thick nickel and is engraved with a square. The other's the size of a triple-thick dime and has a triangle. I keep it in my hand and pull out a piece of paper.

Every Seventh

I put a stack of crackers atop a passerby. The woman cried, "Thank you, pal! Nice hat!"

After you've solved this puzzle, place a representative of the item into locker 207 by Monday morning. In addition, please keep the enclosed coin (and ones to follow) in a safe, accessible place. Remember, this is all secret. We're depending on you.

Depending on me? A twelve-year-old kid who gets into trouble? If it's so important, someone should ask the president. Or the Secret Service. Or even Matti, who's a lot more trustworthy than I am. She knew about my tenth birthday present for a month and wouldn't tell me even when I squeezed her knee in the way that makes her claw at my eyeballs.

But someone's trusting me, and if it's The Legend, I'm all over it.

I put the coin in my underwear drawer on top of the mystery math sheet with the sequence that's still driving me nuts. I flop onto my bed and look at the paper with the new puzzle, if you can call it that. It's just a headline and some weird sentences.

"Okay," I say to Curry. "I'll pretend it's a puzzle, but it's so not a puzzle. Read it, Curry."

Great. Now I'm asking a dog to read. But whoever claimed this is a puzzle is also nuts. Who would mistake some crackers for a hat? And what's with the headline? Did the person put a stack of crackers on the head of every seventh person who passed him? I'm surprised no one slugged him in the nose.

"Wouldn't you slug him in the nose?" I ask Curry.

She looks up and wags her tail.

"No, you'd shake the crackers off your head and eat them."

I shake my own head. At least the first puzzle was something I recognized. Teachers always throw math sequences at us. Maybe The Legend did that to get me all confident because they knew this puzzle was gonna smack all the confidence out of me.

I should pretend it's like math, that there's some logic to it. The only logic, though, is in the directions, which tell me to put a representative of the solution into the locker. But what's a representative? Like in the House of Representatives?

I picture rushing off to Washington, DC, grabbing a member of Congress, and shoving him into locker 207. Which is physically possible. Maybe not the kidnapping, but the shoving.

Last year I took a dare and ate my lunch in my locked locker for two days in a row. Principal Wilkins told me I could've suffocated in there, but I don't know how a kid can suffocate when the vents are big enough to wiggle his fingers through. I'm not stupid. I figured if no one let me out, someone would hear me yell and see my fingers.

But they're not looking for a guy shoved into a locker.

"What are they looking for, Curry?"

It'd be so easy to forget this puzzle and go kick around the soccer ball. I grab a Nerf ball from under my bed and glance it off my closet door. Again. And again.

And a few minutes later I'm outside, kicking a regulation soccer ball against the garage door. Can I really figure out this puzzle? Kick. Kick. Kick. And if I can't? Kick. Kick. Kick. Or what if this isn't The Legend and the oaf's punking me? Kick. Kick. Kick. No. I never gave him my combination, and he wouldn't know the one to locker 207 unless he had 207 in sixth grade. Kick. Kick. Kick. Or shoved the envelope through the vents. But would it fit? Kick. Kick. Kick. Wait. He's an oaf, and oafs like him don't write puzzles. They steal them. If I look on the internet and the puzzle's not there, then he couldn't have sent it.

I kick my soccer ball inside, head upstairs, and great. Of all times to be banned from the computer. If I look for just one minute, my parents won't know. Unless they have it rigged with Travis traps.

Forget it. I pick up the puzzle again.

Every Seventh

It's underlined, so it has to be a title, right? But titles have stuff in common with the words below. This one doesn't. Maybe it's a clue. Every seventh what? Every seventh word?

Every Seventh

I put a stack of crackers atop a passerby. The woman cried, "Thanks, pal! Nice hat!"

Do I count the words in the title? That would give me *of* and *cried*. Without the title, *atop* and *pal*. A pal is a thing, but I won't exactly find lots of volunteers to get stuffed into Locker 207. Unless the *representative* part means I'm supposed to get a mini pal. Like a doll or something. Great. Now I have to go to the toy store and risk someone seeing me buy a Barbie.

But wait. I'd need to use *atop*, too. If I push the words together . . .

Ofcried? Atoppal? They aren't in the dictionary. Neither are the letter combos I'd make if I started with the first words instead of the seventh.

Every seventh. Every seventh. Not words. Letters maybe?

I start with the title, then write down every seventh

letter. E-P-C-C-O-E-W-I-K-C. Nothing. What if I ditch the title?

Maybe start with the seventh letter after the headline?

T. Then R.

There are lots of "tr" words. But I need a vowel next.

A! Then S. H.

Keep going.

C-A-N.

"Trash can, Curry. I did it! An item!"

I need a locker-sized trash can. How big is a locker?

When my backpack's loaded, it barely fits in sideways. I cram my backpack with junk from underneath my bed, then I measure it against the bathroom trash cans. I measure it against the bedroom ones. My mom must have this thing for bigger-than-locker trash cans.

Now what? I can't exactly say, "Excuse me, Mom, but will you take me to the store, stay in the car, don't look at what I buy, and don't ask any questions?" That's gonna fly. And with my enslavement this weekend, I can't go riding my bike wherever I need.

I have only one choice.

CHAPTER
■ 10 ■

Day two of detention. I wait in the driveway with my backpack full of cans and my bicycle resting against my side. When Mrs. Pinchon pulls up, I walk my bike to her window and try to ignore her question mark eyebrows. "I was wondering if I might be able to ride home. My legs need to pedal."

She looks at the cloudy-dark sky. "We'll see." She helps me load my bike into her pickup, and I breathe for the first time in a minute.

I plan to wait until after school to ask about leaving early. "In case you're curious," I say, apparently forgetting to tell my mouth about the plan, "I have an important errand to run."

"You do, do you?"

"And it's always safer to ride home before rush hour, so I was sort of wondering . . ."

"If we could end our arrangement early tonight?"

I smile. "And to make up for it, you can pick me up Monday morning."

"Hmm."

Why'd I offer that? I bite the tip of my tongue to remind my mouth to shut up. It's easier for people to say no if you ask too much.

She ignores my request all morning. After school, still nothing. She does have a bottle of chocolate milk and a poppy seed muffin waiting for me. She must've remembered the poppy seeds in the moon cookies. But it'd be nicer if she paroled me from prison forty-five minutes early. Half hour, even.

I eat my muffin and watch the sweep-second hand of the wall clock spin round and round. The minutes fly. Like a hippopotamus.

I have zero to do except wonder about our baseball game. And stare at the clouds, hanging as heavy as they did this morning. And ignore the rumbling that isn't my stomach.

Mrs. Pinchon looks at the sky. The flicker of lightning

doesn't escape her either. She stays quiet, but the rain speaks enough. It bashes the window and dashes my chance at getting the trash can today.

Fine. I open my social studies book, and twenty minutes later I finish reading about Mesopotamia. I haul out my math book and work the five problems. Almost four o'clock and everything's so quiet. Where'd the rain go?

I work on a paragraph for English and my piece of paper gets brighter. I dare to look up. The sun's sending out some beams. I finish the paragraph. Four twenty-five. I'm done with my homework. Time to unbite my tongue. "Mrs. Pinchon?"

"Travis?"

"I just finished my homework. Every bit. Okay if I take my books to my locker?"

She nods then glances out the window.

Say something, Mrs. Pinchon. Say I can leave.

"Uh, Travis?" she says when I'm almost at the door. "Tell me about this errand of yours."

This is the worst test a principal can give a kid. If she's testing whether I can follow blue envelope directions and I tell her anything, I fail. If I refuse to speak, I fail. If I lie, I fail, but I do get to go. And who would it hurt?

I don't stop to think about that. "Well," I say, stalling

for inspiration that includes a semitruth. "I promised I'd pick up this thing at the store. And if I don't go today, I might have to break my promise."

Which is sort of true. When I put the circle in the locker, it was a kind of promise I'd follow the rules.

"And your parents know about this?"

They should, according to Rule #5, but I don't say that. "My dad doesn't. He's in Japan."

"And your mom?" She pushes the phone toward me.

I hate this. I punch in my home number and talk before the answering machine picks up. "Hi, Mom. It's me." I pause like I'm waiting for her to talk. "Remember that errand?" Pause. "Mrs. Pinchon says I can do it. Okay?" Pause. "Thanks, Mom." Pause. "Yeah, I'll be careful." Pause. "Bye." I hang up as the leave-your-name-at-the-beep message ends.

Mrs. Pinchon stares me in the eye. For too long.

I can't stand this. "Am I supposed to do something else?"

She takes in a deep breath. "I'll page Mr. McKenzie to fetch your bicycle from my truck, then I'll see you bright and early tomorrow morning. Monday morning, too."

I almost feel like hugging her, even with the extra detention. "Thanks, Mrs. Pinchon." I give her my best smile, and she gives a half one right back.

It's a five-minute ride to the office supply store, where they should have small trash cans, then a ten-minute ride back home. Even if I take half an hour in the store, I can get back by five thirty, so I ditch going home to leave a real message for my mom.

I pedal fast, dodging some of the little tree branches that fell with all the wind and rain, and I make it to the store in what might be record time.

I race to the trash can aisle. I don't care what this thing looks like as long as it's the cheapest one I can wedge into a locker. There's a plain black one and a cooler white one with a swinging lid, but it's more expensive. I run the black one over to the ruler aisle. *Cha-ching!* It's small enough. I measured my stuffed backpack yesterday. Checkout time.

I hit a couple display staplers, pass the pens, spin in an office chair, and . . . wait. I'm in an office supply store. With computers. Without parents. With at least twenty-five more minutes. And . . . *cha-ching* again! One computer is loaded with Son of Crash.

I move Crash Junior around the third bend. My hand rumbles with the amazing new audio until Crash crashes, right before I get to the fourth level. I try again. And again and . . .

How much longer do I have? I check the clock on the computer next to me. Five-twenty!

I practically throw my money at the cashier, unchain my bike, and race out of there. Not only do I need to beat the clock, I need to beat that next wave of thunderclouds gathering closer than I'd like. I head toward the horizon, my legs churning as fast as they can.

They pedal me off the busy road into a neighborhood street about three blocks before Matti's house. I'm still more than five minutes from home. Five minutes under normal circumstances. The way my legs are burning, I'm not riding like normal.

I pass Matti's, churn uphill, round the corner, look behind me to cross into the next neighborhood. No cars. Go. Go. Go!

I cruise down the next street. I'm gonna make it.

Three more turns. One turn. Pedal. Pedal.

Two turns. Ped—

No!

I'm lying in the street, my helmet covering most of my sight. I sit up and move my arms and legs. I look into my backpack and check the trash can. Nothing's broken except the skin on my elbow and forearm. It's all scraped and bloody. Maybe I can make it home on time. Or maybe my mom's late. Maybe she got caught in rain-slow traffic and . . .

Doesn't matter. Half my front tire is hanging like wet toilet paper from a tree. I raise the handlebars, mostly with my good arm, and try to run my bike home on its back wheel. I hobble it down the driveway just as my mom closes the back door behind her.

By now she'll be heading up the stairs, calling my name. I can come in behind her and say I've been outside, or not. No hiding my torn shirt, the blood, and the rip I just found on the side of my pants.

"I'm down here, Mom," I call with as little energy as possible.

Curry even senses my problems because she doesn't charge me. She just circles around and licks my hand.

My mom's barefoot, but still has on her work clothes when she comes into the kitchen. "Travis! What happened?"

"I'm fine. I didn't see the branch in the street and flew over the handlebars."

She goes into Nurse Mom mode and forgets to ask why I was on my bike. She won't forget for long, though.

"So, Mrs. Pinchon let me load my bike onto her pickup this morning," I say to get this over with. "And my legs were itching to pedal after being in prison, and I knew I couldn't go to the baseball game because that's part of my punishment, so I went to the store to get something for school and . . ."

In the time it takes her to tear open a Band-Aid, her face changes from Nurse Mom to Judge Mom. "And Mrs. Pinchon knew where you were going?"

"Sort of."

"And you called me so I knew where you'd be?"

"I tried, but you weren't home yet and—"

"Of course I wasn't home yet. But you do know my work number and my cell."

"I was gonna be home on time."

"You're twelve, Travis. Not twenty-two." She screws the top back onto the ointment tube. "Even if you were, you'd still need to let someone know where you're going. Always."

"I know." I open the next Band-Aid wrapper. "I will. I promise."

She looks straight into my eyes like they're trying to cement that promise into my brain, then she stays really quiet. Worried quiet. Sad quiet. Like when she remembers my grandparents.

I'd rather be banned from TV for life than listen to this type of quiet.

"So," she says, but nothing follows. She finishes the bandaging, and I follow her to the kitchen. She gets out a Diet Coke. "So, what should we do with you?"

I let out a quiet laugh. "Mrs. Pinchon said something like that before I got detention."

"I think I might like Mrs. Pinchon." My mom pulls some tuna steaks from the refrigerator, but she's not smiling much, and it's my fault.

If I'd actually called her, we might be laughing now.

But I sort of make her laugh during dinner when I get up, jump twice, pretend I'm flying in a plane, and stomp my feet. Then I pull her arm until she does the Stamp Dance with me, the one Grandpa Sam made up to get me interested in the stamp collection he started for me.

And by the time dinner's done, she hasn't heaped on extra punishment. She tells me we'll fix my bike this weekend, then she sends me and Curry up to my room, which is fine. Because I need to figure out how to sneak a trash can into a school locker I'm not supposed to open.

CHAPTER

▪11▪

It's nearly midnight, and I still don't know what to say when Mrs. Pinchon's eyebrows ask why I'm bringing a trash can to school. I want to use her line, "Things aren't always as they appear," but that'll work only if I dress up the trash can in a wig and moustache and . . .

Bingo! I tell the plan to my voice-activated tape recorder in case I forget by morning, which I don't. I take care of everything and get ready for school.

"Is that what you bought yesterday?" my mom asks right before I go out the door.

"Yeah," I say, holding up the gift-wrapped trash can. "A trash can for someone-on-a-team." Not a lie. The

Legend has to be the ultimate team, right?

"I hope this isn't about where they can stuff themselves."

"Nope. They asked for it."

"Asked for it? As in payback?"

"As in, they requested it."

She sips her coffee, and I'm out the door before she asks anything else.

In less than a minute Mrs. Pinchon pulls up. She stares at the gift-wrapped can. "Is that from your errand yesterday?"

"Yeah."

"That, too?" She points to my banged-up arm.

"A bonus." A bonus for lying. "And it kept waking me up." I yawn.

We both stay quiet except when I yawn three more times. She notices, and when we get to school, she gives me permission to "walk off my sleepies for ten minutes." That means I can dump the trash can into locker 207. Her permission came almost too easily, like she knew I needed to do that. Which might be possible. Some adult needs to be in charge of The Legend.

It'd be cooler if The Legend were only kids, but we can't drive to get places, we don't have big money for extreme Events, and we don't have access to school locker combinations.

I open the 207 lock, trying not to let the middle number bother me. But I want to scream for someone to explain why it's 23. And why this trash can doesn't quite fit through the opening. I kick it until it does. Now where's my blue envelope? If I pay the locker what it asks for, shouldn't it pop out an envelope like a gumball machine would? It practically did last time.

I kick the locker shut, jam on the lock, and try to figure out how to kill the next seven minutes. There's nothing but dark classrooms up here. And kid voices downstairs. I follow their noise, then I lose them. Did they come from Mr. McKenzie's supply closet? No one's there.

Now what? Idea. That case of toilet paper I lugged up to the pipe room. I asked Mr. McKenzie how long it would last. He's gonna let me know when it's gone, but I go check how many we've used so far. I stick my head way inside the box. Whoa. All ninety-six rolls in two days? There's a whole lot of bathrooming going on.

That's all the fun I can stand. I take the long way back to Mrs. Pinchon's office and open one of those library books she brought in. It's about a kid who hates school and likes basketball, and it's not too bad. At least it's good enough that when I hear the first bell, I realize Mrs. Pinchon hasn't needed to look at me funny.

"You're dismissed, Mr. Raines," she says. "Until after school." Why'd she rub it in?

I put the book back on the stack, pick up my backpack and—

Dernck! Dernck! Dernck! Dernck! Dernck!

Mr. McKenzie barges right in, looking like he's about to spit fire. As I leave, he glares at me like I'm to blame for the world's problems.

I'm in class for about two minutes when the intercom crackles. "Travis Raines," the voice says, "please report to Mrs. Pinchon's office."

I get all this "Ooh, Travis. What'd you do this time? Ooh, Travis. In trouble again? Ooh, Travis. Climb any good roofs lately?"

I raise my eyebrows. I grin. But it's only from habit. I know things I do make people say the Ooh-Travis stuff, and mostly it's fun, but not now. Maybe I'm sick of being the troublemaker. Or maybe I know I'm about to get blamed for something I didn't do. Or maybe, with that look Mr. McKenzie shot me, I need to worry I'm out of The Legend's blue-envelope game forever.

I pass the boys' bathroom. It has a wet floor sign in front, and the door's taped off.

I pass another one nearer to Mrs. Pinchon's office. Same—

"This is a message for all students." It's Mr. Wilkins over the loudspeaker.

My stomach starts putting things together. I slow down to get a preview of why I'm walking to the assistant principal in charge of discipline again.

"The next time you are in the halls," the voice says, "you'll notice that all the boys' bathrooms are closed for servicing. They will be reopened as the day goes on. Meanwhile we have marked some of the girl's rest rooms for male usage. Please pay careful attention to the signs. Thank you for your cooperation."

I'll cooperate. I'll burst through Mrs. Pinchon's door and tell her I'm not to blame for anything bathroom related except helping Mr. McKenzie carry cases of toilet paper.

When I get there, though, she's standing at the door. Waiting for me. We don't even sit.

"It appears," she says, her hypnotizing necklace swaying back and forth, "that someone or some *ones* thought it hilarious to drop a roll of toilet paper into each of the boys' toilets. It also appears that all the toilet paper came from the case you stored in the plumbing access closet. Now, I don't know about you, but we don't go around announcing where staff or students can find ninety-six rolls of toilet paper." She stares like I'm supposed to confess.

I shake my head. "I didn't do it. I wouldn't do it."

"As they say in crime, you had opportunity, knowledge, and motive."

I let that sink in for a second. "Okay. I knew where the toilet paper was, and maybe I had time this morning to run to every bathroom, but why would I do that?"

She points to my little table.

"No, Mrs. Pinchon. I know I was stupid to hang off the roof. I might not love being here, but I wouldn't retaliate by flushing whole toilet paper rolls. I wouldn't retaliate, period."

She looks at me like I'm pure evil. "Who said anything about flushing them?"

"Isn't that how the toilets overflowed?"

She takes half a step closer. "Who said anything about them overflowing?"

"Why else would the two bathrooms I passed be taped shut with wet floor signs?"

She backs off. "Good thing your logic is correct, Mr.

Raines. Most toilets did overflow, causing much trouble for the maintenance staff and, I'm certain, much expense to our school."

"Should I help Mr. McKenzie?" I ask, praying I won't need to plunge my hands into toilets.

"That won't be necessary." Mrs. Pinchon's face looks less threatening, but I'm definitely not out of trouble. And I need to get out of trouble. I need an alibi. Or someone else to—

"Knowledge!" I almost shout. "I am guilty. Guilty of opening my big mouth."

"Explain, Mr. Raines."

"Wednesday at the money machines. I was complaining how my arms hurt from carrying the toilet paper, and I especially complained about taking that box upstairs. Lots of people were around me. Anyone could've heard that." Anyone like Randall. "And opportunity," I say.

"Go on."

"This morning I heard kids' voices in the hallway before I came back to your office, but I didn't see who they belonged to. And I know the door to the pipe closet was unlocked because I just wanted to see how much toilet paper was used."

"And these kids? Their motive?" she asks.

"I don't know, but you've got to believe me. I'm not lying. I may get into trouble a lot, but I don't do stuff that's destructive."

She finally breaks her stare. "I have no proof, but if I find some, you'll be the first to know." She hands me a return-to-class pass. "I'll see you after school. And Travis? You are on notice. Everyone will be watching out for you. One more slip and it only gets worse."

CHAPTER
■ 12 ■

Last year The Legend started the Friday Lunch Shuffle, where we're assigned to eat with other people we'd almost never sit with. I usually like it, but today I want to be with Matti and Kip and complain about being accused of something I'd never ever do.

At my table for the day, there's a girl who thinks she's too good for us; three other girls who are excited to be together; Cambridge, who's the smartest kid in our grade; and George, a new kid on our soccer team this year. Karl, one of the oafs, comes in last and gives my shoulder a shove. I start to slug him one, but I don't need a third strike. "What?"

"Nothing," he says, backing off. "I was going to congratulate you but forget it."

"Huh?"

"The toilets? We all know it was you, Johnny Flood."

Now I really want to slug him. "Airtight alibi."

"You did it with an alibi? Pure genius, Johnny boy."

Now everyone at the table's looking at me. "I. Didn't. Do it." I clamp my teeth on to my lunch bag, rip the side an inch, ease up, and pull out my sandwich. I manage to talk to George about soccer and stop myself from asking Cambridge if he's in The Legend. The whole time I keep glaring at Karl from the corner of my eye, silently daring him to do something evil when I'm in detention and I truly have an airtight alibi. I swear he and Randall are the bad guys.

Even so, I have a decent time the rest of lunch until the loudspeaker announces that the bathrooms are open again. Then every kid either applauds or boos me for pulling the prank.

I stand and pretend to take a bow, but I'm really looking for the only people who will believe me. I don't see Kip, but Matti's table is on the way to the garbage cans. I grab my trash, and everyone I pass taunts me. Except Matti. She gets up and walks with me.

"I didn't do it," I say.

"I didn't think you did."

"You didn't think?" I slam my bag into the can. "You should *know* I wouldn't do it."

"Travis. Calm down. That's what I meant. You're the fun guy. Not the evil guy."

"So why do I get blamed for everything?"

"You know why," she says. "You draw attention to yourself, so you're a perfect target. And you never get into big trouble, so people don't feel guilty about aiming at you."

"Not into big trouble?" I say. "What about detention in Mrs. Pinchon's office?"

"You've gotta admit," Matti says, "even you saw that coming."

I don't want to nod, so I look past her shoulder.

Kip's heading toward us. "You didn't do it, did you?" he says.

I feel my jaw turn to iron. "Do you even have to ask?"

He looks away. "Sorry."

Matti puts a hand on his shoulder. Great. I didn't mean to bring them together even more. But I especially didn't mean to sound nasty, especially not to Kip, who practically flogs himself if he steps on an ant. "I'm just frustrated. Sorry I yelled. Did I yell?"

Kip shakes his head.

"A little," Matti says. "But the good news is it's Friday."

"Which means I spend the next two days as slave labor inside my own house."

Matti shakes her head. "What I mean is by Monday you'll be old news, and life and baseball will go on."

Right after school I'm at my locker. Jammed mostly through the vent is a smaller, non-shiny envelope, the same blue as the one Mrs. Bloom had for the Legend Event. But this one has my name on it. The next puzzle? If it is, they can't believe I'm Johnny Flood.

There are lots of eyes in the hallway, so I slide the envelope into my backpack. As I go into Mrs. Pinchon's office, she leaves "for a second." I open the envelope.

If you want more blue envelopes, play by our seven rules plus all of the school's.
This is your first and last warning.

My teeth vibrate. I've never gotten a yellow card in a soccer game. I play hard but fair. I don't cheat. I don't hog the ball. I don't trip anyone or even try. The goal is to win, and that means being a team and working together and not accusing innocent people.

I bite on my finger to stop my teeth from shaking. "Ahh!"

Great. Mrs. Pinchon comes in mid-scream. "Travis?"

"I'm sorry," I say, "but I'm really angry."

She sit-leans at the front of her desk. "Go on."

"Why? Nothing's gonna change."

She looks as if she'd lean there all year, waiting for me to talk.

"For one thing, why'd you have to summon me over the intercom? I can handle people calling me Johnny Flood, but calling me over the intercom? That makes me look guilty."

Mrs. Pinchon wheels her chair from behind her desk to the front. She sits. "When police work to solve a crime," she says, her voice too calm, "they speak with anyone who might have knowledge of or potential involvement in the case. They will bring innocent people into the station to ask them questions in order to get at the truth."

"But you didn't have to handcuff me in front of the whole school."

"You do have a vivid imagination, Mr. Raines."

"Well, it felt like that."

"I understand," she says. "But if you look at it from our perspective, we had good reason to suspect you. You knew about the toilet paper, and Mr. McKenzie saw you with the carton."

"I didn't see him."

"Your head was inside."

"Because it was already empty. That proves I didn't do it."

She shakes her head. "The police could argue you were making sure you used it all. Or you were reaching in for the last rolls."

I throw my hands into the air. "Let people believe what they want. I know the truth."

"Yes, you do," she says. "That's what's important."

Why doesn't it feel that way? "Can I ask you something?"

Mrs. Pinchon has started to roll her chair away, but she turns back.

"If someone like my friend Kip had the same knowledge and opportunity I had, would you have called him over the loudspeaker? Would people be calling him Johnny Flood?"

She doesn't say anything right away. "Fair question."

I should remember phrases like that when I need to stall for an answer.

"Under the exact circumstances? Kip being who he is? It may not be fair, but I have an inkling we'd have handled it differently." She shakes her head. "You have a strong spirit, Travis. You just need to find a way to haul it in a bit."

"Fine." There's not much more I can say.

I pull out my social studies book and wonder what it feels like to be Kip, who would keel over if he dreamed about dumping a single roll of toilet paper into one toilet. How does a person get to be that way? Not that I'd want to be Kip, but maybe knowing how his brain works could help me haul in my spirit. Or kill it, and reinvent me as Travis Raines the Perfect.

And Travis Raines the Perfect would not be filling in the Os in his social studies book with his pencil. Especially if he's on his last chance to stay in The Legend.

I pull out a full eraser—less chance of ripping the page—and make my scribbles invisible. I wish it worked that way in real life. I'd make a fortune selling giant erasers. Just to myself.

At 5:20, Mrs. Pinchon tells me to visit my locker before she takes me home.

The only good thing to come from detention is I finish all my homework for the weekend so I can dump off my books. And yes! There's another envelope. The big shiny kind.

That's gotta mean I'm still in. Right?

CHAPTER
▪13▪

Hoo-hah! We have a puzzle.

It's after dinner, the first chance I have to open this envelope. The second I got home, my mom drove us straight to a new Chinese restaurant. We didn't have the carryout menu, so we ordered there, came home, and ate. And now I have coin number two and a new puzzle.

> I am toward the edge of the river,
> In the midst of the tropical tree,
> At the very start of the island,
> But never inside of the sea.

*Tack a representative of me onto the bulletin board next
to the drama room.*
Deadline: Tuesday, end of school.
Don't let anyone see you do this.

"There's the representative thing again, Curry." We're
on my bedroom floor, and she's leaning against my leg.
"Glad they didn't ask me to tack a trash can onto a bulletin
board."

It could be worse. Watch this answer be *sofa*. How
would I get a sofa up there? A toy sofa? Like from a
dollhouse? Or . . .

I almost slap myself upside the head. "I didn't have
to spend all that money, Curry. Or get into trouble with
Mom. Or ask Mrs. Pinchon for a favor. Or volunteer for
detention Monday morning. I could've shoved a picture
of a trash can into that locker."

At least I won't get into trouble this time, if I can figure
out the answer. But how do I solve this thing? The locker
was easy. It was math. And the trash can? Okay. So I didn't
know how to solve that, but I did it. How'd I do it?

Maybe if I take this one line at a time. *I am toward the
edge of the river.*

What's at the edge of the river? Which river?

The Mississippi? I know that one, the edge of it, too. "Remember, Curry? Remember when Dad took us to the cobblestone levee. We looked at the paddle wheelers and skipped rocks into the river? And I wanted to pretend you were a seeing-eye dog so we could take you to the top of the Arch?"

Bad idea, then. No ideas from the first line of this puzzle now.

Second line: *In the midst of the tropical tree.*

Like a palm tree? With fronds and coconuts? All of which are not on any river I know.

Line three: *At the very start of the island.*

Where does an island start? Where does a bagel start? "Or your water bowl, Curry?"

Line four: *But never inside of the sea.*

Wait a minute. Seas are filled with islands. Islands can have palm trees and rivers. And none of this makes sense. None of it.

If someone wants me in the group, they should yank me from behind, drag me to a deserted room and say, "You're part of The Legend. Now let's have fun." What does solving puzzles prove? I had to qualify to get this far. Shouldn't that be enough?

My hands itch. They want to wad up the paper and

forget all this. For three reasons. One: I am not Cambridge. If people think they're recruiting some genius, they're delusional. Two: If I have to keep a secret from everyone I know—except Curry, who doesn't talk back—we're all in trouble. And I don't want to think about three, that if I can't solve these puzzles then I really must be Johnny Flood the Worthless.

That's what stops me from walking away. Plus someone thinks I'm good enough for this test. And if that someone's The Legend, I'm here.

Maybe my brain'll think of another idea if I'm not thinking about the puzzle. Instead I can . . . what? I can't watch TV or play computer or video games. My mom would play cards if I wanted, but she's all happy on the couch watching her show and reading a magazine at the same time.

I decide to make her happier and ask to start my weekend chores tonight.

She gushes like I gave her a diamond necklace or saved the world from monsoons. And even though I find myself standing at the living room window with a bottle of Windex and a stack of newspaper, which she says wipes the glass cleaner than paper towels, it's not so bad because I'm actually accomplishing what I'm supposed to.

The next morning I power wash the garage door, which I do three times a year to get rid of my soccer ball marks. Next, I pick up the foam packing peanuts I knocked over in the basement last month. That's fun because I launch handfuls of them toward the garbage bag and see how few make it. After lunch my mom gives me a break, and I get to go with her to the airport to pick up my dad, who's coming home from Japan. First we take a detour to the library.

She lets me use the computer there—for school, I tell her. It sort of is. I type The Legend poem into a search engine, which is a waste of time. Most entries for "toward the edge of the river" are from nobody bloggers who walked to the edge of one.

For "tropical trees" I keep picturing monkeys until I discover they might jump into the sea if they're in danger. Other birds and animals fit every line, but which one would I choose?

All this research is hurting my brain, but I can't exactly let my mom catch me playing computer games. Idea! And it's school related. The Legend's web page!

It's no secret there's a link on the Lauer Middle School home page to a Legend page. It's just the group symbol, and all it says is "The Legend Lives!" But what if that's not all?

I pull up the black page with the blue words and symbol. I move the cursor around and click every piece of blue just in case. Nothing. But it feels good to click and click and click some more. And I keep clicking even when my mom calls my name and I swivel around.

She's waving her cell phone. "Dad's plane landed. Let's go."

I turn back to sign off the computer and—

Wow! There's more on The Legend screen. A whole mess of writing. How'd it get here?

"Mom. Two minutes, please?"

The way she shakes her head, I can't change her mind.

"Can I at least print?"

"C'mon."

I take a quick look at the screen, long enough to read:

It was all Mrs. Blumeyer's fault.
The pranks.
The punishment.
The Legend.

CHAPTER
▪14▪

No matter how creative I get all weekend, I can't convince my mom to let me on the computer. Then when I try to concentrate on the puzzle, I can't get my mind off birds and animals. At least the chores don't make me completely crazy. Just crazy enough so that I'm dreaming a chimp and I are painting skylight glass when the phone wakes me up.

It's 6:28 on Monday morning, but our phone rings at all sorts of weird hours, with my mom running the engineering business and my dad doing work overseas.

My dad comes to my door, still on the phone, still looking jet-lagged. "Hold on, please." He lowers the phone against his chest. "It's Mrs. Pinchon. She can't pick you up this morning."

"Hoo-hah. I can ride my bike."

My dad shakes his head, barely able to hold it up. "Someone needs to take you. Mom's leaving in a minute, so it's either me or some Mr. McKenzie, who's going in early to open up. You know him?"

"He's fine," I say. For a snitch.

Why can't my dad be wide awake? Or even better, why can't Mrs. Pinchon send that Lookout Transportation Services bus with the couch seats? I guess this isn't reward time.

I wait outside with my bike, but when Mr. McKenzie pulls up in his black sports car, I know it won't fit. Before I turn back to the garage, though, he pops open the trunk. "Let's do this," he says. Then he maneuvers blankets and ropes to protect both my bike and the car.

We get in, and the way he's smiling at me, I know I won't like what he's about to say.

"So, first thing, Travis, we need to clear the air and discuss toilet paper," he says. "Not how many times I had to sink elbow-deep into germ-ridden toilets . . ."

And blah-blah-blah. I want to cover my ears and not listen to the rest of his accusations.

"But after I told Mrs. Pinchon I saw your head in that box, I realized something. I was fixing a sink in the front hall boys' room right before that, so unless you're Superman, I told her, there's no way you could have personally hit that bathroom."

"I didn't. Not any of them."

"Sorry I jumped to conclusions, kid. If there's anything I can do to make it up to you . . ."

"You can," I say, getting an idea. "And no germs involved. Just tell me what you know about The Legend."

"Oh no," he says. "You're not getting those secrets from me."

"You know their secrets?"

He laughs. "Actually, none at all."

"But you help set up for Events, right? Someone has to tell you what to do."

"That information all comes in blue envelopes or through e-mail. Anonymously. And even if I had vital information—well, I know how to keep big secrets." He shifts in his seat. "So let's just say I owe you one and change the subject."

"Not back to toilet paper."

He laughs again. "How about cars? Do you like this one?"

"It's expensive, isn't it?"

He nods. "Which is why I do home repairs after hours. Tell your parents. I can always use the extra bucks, and there's rarely enough overtime pay at school."

Overtime pay? Did he flood the bathrooms himself so he could work overtime?

I want to ask, but there's no way to do that without sounding like a brat or accusing him or worse. He could deny it then set me up again. I pretend-smile instead.

His sandy brown mustache goes up at the corners, raising his matching goatee, like we're buddies now. Which we're not.

We get to school, and Mr. McKenzie helps me get my bike out, lets me into the building, unlocks Mrs. Pinchon's darkened office, then leaves me there.

I reach for the light switch, but I kinda like it dark. I spin in Mrs. Pinchon's big chair and pretend I'm her laying into Randall. "For making Travis do dangerous deeds, it's time to taste your own medicine. You'll climb the flagpole and balance on top, standing on one leg for three hours, drinking two gallons of water. And you're not allowed to pee. Then you'll leap onto the school roof and run across the top in five seconds or get mauled by a pack of wolves. The only way down is to jump, so if you break every bone in your body, it's your own fault."

That'd serve him right. Not only for taking Kip's cap, but for elbowing my lunch tray on spaghetti day in fifth grade. When the teachers were looking, he stooped down with the other oafs and pretended to help me clean it up. The only thing he cleaned up was my $5.85 in change. No matter how much I yelled at him, he swore he didn't take it. Marco saw him, though.

My flagpole punishment would make up for him basically harassing me my whole life.

I smile and lay my head on Mrs. Pinchon's desk. Problem. With the lights off and the chair so comfortable, I might fall asleep. I need to move.

I open Mrs. Pinchon's top drawer and use a black Sharpie on a neon orange note.

Mrs. Pinchon,
I went to my locker to get my books for first hour. I'll be back in five minutes.
Travis

I jam the note into my pocket. There's no neon orange anything on top of her desk. She'll know I opened her drawer. I write the same note with my stuff.

I figure I have at least seven minutes.

The fastest way to my locker means turning left. I turn right and walk to the end of the hall then turn left and . . . Why am I walking? The halls are deserted, and Mr. McKenzie's my new buddy. I jog down the hall. I sprint up the back stairs. I race a half lap around, then slide down the handrail of the stairs on the other side. I zoom around the school two more times and slide down the banister four more and see the librarian coming out of the library. I slow down until she clears the hallway. Idea!

I slip into the media center, access The Legend page, then click everywhere. I click the corners, I click the sides, I click every blue letter and every corner of the symbol. I even look away like I did on Saturday when I happened to hit the right spot. Nothing. I need a system.

I start at the lower left-hand corner and click in a straight line across the bottom of the screen. I move slightly higher and click another straight line. And another. And another. And . . .

Bingo! Black screen. Lots of blue writing.

It was all Mrs. Blumeyer's fault.
The pranks.
The punishment.

The Legend.

If she hadn't been such a legendary teacher, herself . . .

if she'd disappeared midyear instead of announcing her departure two months before the fact . . .

then none of this would have happened,

and none of this would exist.

For better or for worse.

THE PLAN

The seven students involved called it The Blu Plan, but they never agreed on one best way to persuade Mrs. Blu to finish out the school year. They did agree to disagree and to act simultaneously upon their disagreements. One dewy November morning long before sunrise, each of the seventh graders showed up ready to carry out his or her mission.

THE PRANKS

Prank #1 Perpetrated by Amy Williams (now a business owner), who wrapped all the grammar and reading books from Mrs. Blu's room in blue construction paper and arranged them on the grass outside the classroom window so they spelled DON'T LEAVE, MRS. BLU.

Prank #2 Perpetrated by Pat Bryan (now our assistant district attorney), who attached a set of blue "jail bars" across the window of her classroom door.

Prank #3 Perpetrated by Chase Maclin (now a singer/songwriter), who broke into the broadcast room and programmed an original song, "The Blumeyer Blues," to play continuously over the school speaker system.

Prank #4 Perpetrated by Lydia March (now a White

House reporter), who constructed a blue cage around Mrs. Blu's desk and chair, complete with door and lock.

Prank #5 Perpetrated by Susan Stein (now a university math professor), who set one thousand clear plastic, water-filled cups outside the school's front door, then added blue food coloring to strategic cups so the word *stay* was visible from above.

Prank #6 Perpetrated by Dan Fletcher (now a video game creator), who programmed the school computer network so all screens booted up with a solid blue background and the continuously streaming words MRS. BLU MUST STAY!

Prank #7 Perpetrated by Griffin Barnett (now an IT consultant), who plastered the halls with 500 blue-paper, photocopied Wanted posters of Mrs. Blu.

THE PROBLEM

Prank #1 The morning dew caused the color of the construction paper to bleed on all the book covers.

Prank #2 Removal of the jail bars left nail holes in the window frames.

Prank #3 Breaking the lock on the door cost hundreds of dollars in repair.

Prank #4 When removed, the cage wire left telltale snags in the carpet.

Prank #5 Blue food coloring stained the concrete walkway.

Prank #6 The district technology expert spent hours getting back into the computer system.

Prank #7 The litter problem resulted in overtime work for custodians.

THE FALLOUT

It helped that the intentions were noble and the actions, creative. By the time the administration identified all the perpetrators, Mrs. Blumeyer had decided to stay the rest of the year with one condition: the seven students would work with her to create what was to become The Legend.

LOGIN NAME_____
PASSWORD_____

I can't stop smiling. The rumors are true. Chase Maclin is an original Legend. And me! I'm exactly like those kids who tried to do something good but messed up. I need to find out more.

Maybe I'm not supposed to but . . . No one's around. I type my own name into the login space and try my school password. Nothing. I keep my name and type *TheBluPlan* for the password. Nothing. Now what?

I look around. The clock! 7:20. I can't have been gone for fifteen minutes.

I can only pray Mrs. Pinchon hasn't gotten to school yet.

CHAPTER

▪15▪

I run toward the office. And stop. If she's back and I come in without my books . . .

Back upstairs to my locker. Right, left, right. Click! I grab my stuff, slam the locker, shut the lock, and slide down the banister one more time. It's faster. I round the corner, ready with an excuse, but I get lucky.

The lights are still off in Mrs. Pinchon's office. "Alone, alone, alone," I say to the walls.

"Five minutes?" The voice bellows from near the coatrack.

I whip my head toward her desk.

Her chair creeps around. Fingertips. Chin. Pendant. Drawn-on eyebrows. Busted.

"I've been sitting here for seven," she says.

"I didn't think you were—"

"Here?" she says. "Remember, Travis, things aren't always as they appear."

No kidding. "I wasn't trying to take advantage, Mrs. Pinchon. My legs got crazy and needed to stretch. And the computer. I had to use one, and I didn't want to touch yours without permission. And I lost track of time. You can look in the bathroom," I joke. "No flooding."

She doesn't move. I wish she'd yell at me.

My eyeballs orbit, looking for a place to land. They find the window and cars going down the street. "Sorry you couldn't pick me up today," I say. "Everything all right?"

"Everything's fine." Then she says nothing again.

Has everything been fine all along? Was this a test? And I failed? "Should I stay after again today?"

She taps her fingertips to her chin. "Let's just say your time this morning isn't your own."

It hasn't been my own since last Wednesday. But I stay quiet.

"I assume you have paper and pencil in your backpack."

"Yes, ma'am."

"How about a pen? Do you have a pen? Pens are nicer."

"Yes, I have a pen."

"And don't you think it was good of Mr. McKenzie to pick you up this morning?"

I get it now. "Yes, ma'am," I say. "So it would be the right thing to write him a really nice thank-you note."

She gives me a big fake smile, then clicks on the lights.

Instead of ripping the holes of the paper, I open my notebook to get out two sheets. It would behoove me to write a thank-you note to Mrs. Pinchon, too. I have no clue what to thank her for besides the snacks, but by the time I finish, I thank her for understanding how a boy's legs need to move, for letting me out early on Thursday, for smiling at me sometimes, for letting me go to The Legend Event, and for not suspending me to begin with.

I'm writing the *V* in *Sincerely, Travis* when the first bell rings.

I expect her to tell me to finish and leave, but she sits still, fingertips at her chin. "You've been here these few days, Travis," she finally says, "but I feel I barely know you. Before you go, tell me something about yourself that you haven't told me yet."

Why not? If I get her to like me, maybe she'll give me an extra chance sometime. Maybe The Legend will, too. "Like, what do you want to know?"

"I know you have a dog and no brothers or sisters. You like moon cookies and soccer and riding your bike. But what else do you like? What else do you do?"

I don't know. "Normal stuff. My mom and dad had me doing chores all weekend, and I'm still banned from our computer, which is why I needed to use one in the library this morning."

"I understand." She waits for more.

What kind of honest and decent thing could I tell an assistant principal in charge of discipline? Something tame. Something boring. Something besides hating Randall. "There's really not much else. But I'm great at power washing the garage door, and I can cook a little, and, oh, I have a small stamp collection." That sounds really tame.

She smiles. "I have some stamps, too. And I also like to cook and grow vegetables."

"Oh," I say, trying to think of something else to get rid of the weirdness that comes when teachers and principals start sounding like normal people. "And people don't usually know I'm pretty good at reading maps."

"Ah, like the fire escape map."

"Road maps, too, which my parents say is ironic because I'm not so great at following directions."

She laughs. "If I ever need a navigator, I'll know who to call."

It's even weirder that any principal might call for my help. I smile anyway and hold up the letters. "Should I mail these?"

The second bell rings.

"I'll take care of them." She takes the letters and hands me a class pass. "You're excused, Mr. Raines," she says, almost as if she's disappointed.

Maybe she's lonely at home and this is all the company she gets. Maybe I should visit her occasionally. Maybe I'm going nuts.

I grab my backpack. "Bye, Mrs. Pinchon." I head out the door, then I turn around. "Being in here with you hasn't been as bad as I thought."

"Things aren't always as they appear, are they?" She smiles at me.

I give her my best smile back.

But her words are sticking with me. Things aren't always as they appear. What's not always as it appears? The answer to the puzzle?

I stop short of my math class and look down the hallway. Deserted! I pull the puzzle back out. Quickly. Mrs. Pinchon put a time on my class pass.

I am toward the edge of the river,
In the midst of the tropical tree,
At the very start of the island,
But never inside of the sea.

I push birds and monkeys from my head and walk into class. And when I hand the pass to my teacher, I get more jeers. Why'd Mrs. Pinchon keep me late? Matti was right. Everyone would've forgotten if I'd kept under the radar, but this puts neon lights around my head.

No one would believe me if I tell them it's all good, so I play my normal character and grin and slink into my seat while the teacher wisely ignores me. I wish everyone else would, but the teasing follows me all day, and shoves puzzle solving from my mind, until science.

Mrs. Bloom's explaining biotic and abiotic factors in the ecosystem, and I totally understand those. Last week in Mrs. Pinchon's office I read ahead. So instead of listening, I write the important words from the puzzle.

River - toward edge
Tree - midst (middle)
Island - start
Sea - not in

I need to forget nature and think about . . . what? What? I can't think about anything because Mrs. Bloom's voice keeps breaking my concentration. I want to shout for her to be quiet, that I already understand all this. The biotic factors are the living organisms, like the trees and monkeys and birds that've been driving me crazy. The abiotic factors are the nonliving things, like minerals and soil and weather. Idea!

I've been over all the biotic answers in my mind. What if this is an abiotic answer? I poke and push at the paper with my pen. The paper came from a tree. But it's not living anymore. Does that make it abiotic now? I poke my pen on the paper again and again and too much. Great. Now the ink's leaking out.

I entertain myself by moving the pen point over the little ink river on the paper. And I start writing *river* with the puddle. *I am toward the edge of the river*. Not the biotic river. The abiotic river. The word on the paper. With abiotic letters.

An *r*! It's toward the edge of the word *river* and in the midst of the word *tree*. No *r* in island, so that's not the answer, but maybe I'm on to something.

Next letter. *I*. At the very start of *island*. Toward the edge of *river*. Not in sea. Not in *tree* either. Wait. What kind of tree? Tropical tree! With an *i* in its midst! The answer is *i*.

I am so slow. The puzzle tells you the answer. *"I" am toward the edge of the river.*

"I" am about to beat myself over the head, but who cares now? I did it! With a day to spare. Now to get the answer posted. When? When will there be no eyes in the hall? Now.

I rub my finger across the ink puddle, smear a line onto a clean page, then dot it with my fingerprint. I let it dry before I stuff it into my pocket. Then I raise my inky hands. "Should I go to the bathroom?" I ask. "Or should I use the sinks in here and try not to disturb the class?"

Mrs. Bloom nearly groans, but she points to the door, and in ten giant strides I'm heading upstairs.

The drama room is around the corner at the very end. If I can make it past eight more classroom doors with no eyes around, I'm done with this puzzle.

A kid comes out of the French room, but he passes me going the other way. A teacher turns off her lights—movie time, I guess—but that puts me in a spotlight for a second.

I'm just a room away. When I get there, in one motion I'll stop, look for eyes, grab a—

Great. Why didn't I bring a thumbtack or a nail or a javelin or something with a point? There are no extras on the bulletin board. Just tacks holding up the cast list, practice schedule, costume information, meeting that was . . . last week! I untack that paper and start to crumple it. But what if it's a Legend assignment from someone else?

No reason why the old note and mine can't share. I fan the two papers and tack them together, then I'm off to the bathroom.

The thing about ink is you can't exactly wash it off with school-strength soap. I get to a point where the ink stops rubbing onto the paper towels.

I should head straight back to science. No way someone had time to spot my *i* and put another puzzle into my locker, but I can't help myself. Even before I spin the lock, I see something barely in the vent. A smaller, non-shiny blue envelope like the warning one. No!

I can't wait. No eyes in the hall. I open it.

You are about to enter greatness. The secrets are about to be revealed. Follow the directions exactly and you will become one of us.
The Legend of Lauer

CHAPTER
▪ 16 ▪

All right! Does this mean I'm totally forgiven? Almost done? Back to normal? When I'm in The Legend, though, I'll never be normal again.

The Legend! It's signed, *The Legend*! And soon I'll know all their secrets.

I soar back to class and don't really care that Mrs. Bloom glares at me when I walk in. I hold up my stained hands. "The ink wouldn't stop rubbing off on the paper towels."

People are snickering. "Good going, Johnny Flood," Randall whispers. He looks to Marco to add to my misery, but Marco shakes his head and stays quiet.

I can ignore the drama because I'm not as big a screw-up as they think. Also because I have more important things to think about, like why I left that new envelope in my locker. What if it's really the next puzzle in disguise?

I write down every word, at least the ones I can remember, so I can start solving—

Wait. The puzzles come with instructions. This note didn't. It's probably just a note.

But it is The Legend! I'm still flying so fast, it doesn't bother me when they announce the winner of the Chase Maclin prize box. Some eighth grader got an MP3 player, a hundred dollar music-download card, every one of Chase's CDs, and one of his guitars, signed. If I'd won, I swear I would've learned how to play the guitar. Then I could've written Chase to tell him how he changed my life, and he would've written back and maybe I'd get to meet him. I wish he'd show up here one day so I could finally see him in person.

My mom claims he baby-sat for me when I was still in my crib and he was in college, but it'd be hard to believe any rock star changed my diapers unless he told me himself.

Right now, though, I'd be satisfied with another puzzle in my locker. There's nothing after school. Nothing in my gym locker either, but at least I'm here, changing for baseball practice even though it'll be hard to concentrate on it. The Legend!

Matti and Kip and I are tossing around the ball before practice, and the sun is shining and the breeze is blowing.

Then an oaf-sized shadow comes around. "Good. You're back." Randall leers at me then thumps ahead to torment Marco.

"Why should he care?" I say to Matti and Kip. "So he can get me in trouble again?"

"That was weird," says Matti.

"I know," Kip says. "Maybe he's hatching an evil, new plot against you, Trav, and it starts with being nice."

"Maybe he actually decided it's time to be nice."

Kip and I stare at Matti like she's nuts.

"Maybe he was being a loser." I toss the ball to her. "You can't trust a guy who snipes at you in science then says nice stuff out here. Either you're my friend or you're not."

"Which means," says Matti, "that I can't make fun of you again or you'll accuse me of being a hypocrite?"

I run to center field, pretending I didn't hear that. I feel Matti and Kip right behind me.

"I know you heard that!" she yells. "He heard that," she says to Kip.

I laugh and go through practice feeling really good about pretty much everything, except for how many questions I have about The Legend.

Me plus curious equals trouble. It did when I almost fell inside the penguin area at the zoo. And it did when I got lost on a field trip to the Missouri Botanical Garden. But that wasn't my fault. The teachers should've either let us in the maze or they shouldn't have pointed out where it started.

It's not my curiosity that's frustrating me when I get up to bat, though. It's my minuscule strike zone. No pitcher can find it, which gives me nothing to swing at. So I walk to first without the satisfaction of hitting something. Three times.

I'm up again, this time with the oaf pitching. If he doesn't give me a ball to hit, I may come to the mound and hit him.

He winds up and pitches, but the ball's too high. I swing anyway. I need to.

"Strike one!"

I wish Mrs. Pinchon had only one strike against me.

Randall hurls it again. This one's almost in my strike zone. I haul off a big swing.

"Strike two!"

How'd I miss that? And what am I missing with the new envelope? Why does it feel like a rerun? Except the signature. Maybe they're messing with my head like Randall the oaf does.

He takes his windup and pitches. I wait on it. Wait on it. Wait on it. It's there. In my zone. I smash the ball right at his oaf gut. I drop the bat. Take a step. Watch for him to get knocked down by the force—

I cannot believe it. He catches it. He wins again.

Third out of the inning.

All the fielders come in to congratulate Randall like he's won the World Series. I tear off my batting helmet.

Coach Ford pulls me aside. "Keep hitting 'em like that, Raines, and you'll be a star."

I smile. I want to say I'd hit 'em like that if I keep getting pitches like that, but I'd be complimenting the oaf.

I grab my glove from the bench, turn around, and Randall's right there.

"Good hit," he says.

"Good pitch," my mouth says before my brain catches up.

"What is it about him?" I run with Kip to take the field. "Why does he pretend to be all nice sometimes?"

Kip shakes his head. "Split personality?"

No. He's devious. He knows how to get everyone else in trouble and make the teachers believe he's the poster boy for Perfect Student of the Year. How does he get away with his oafish stares or almost killing Jackie Muggs in fourth grade or breaking Natalie Levin's leg last year? Why hasn't anyone shipped him off to a juvenile detention center? Why does Marco keep hanging around with him? We should really help Marco get away.

After practice we change in the locker rooms. Then, like usual, we go to our individual hall lockers. In a minute Matti and Kip will come to mine, then we'll ride our bikes together until we each peel off toward our own street.

I tug open my locker, and it's almost like my birthday. Sitting on the shelf, like one shiny blue present, is a new envelope. No one's coming. I unwind the string and unwind, but Matti and Kip round the corner. Gotta get my envelope home. I grab for my backpack, and the envelope slides out of my grasp. Dives to the floor. I plunk my backpack on top of it and—

"Look out!" Don't know what she tripped over, but Matti's suddenly careening into Kip. Who catches her. And gives me time to get the envelope into the backpack.

When I look up, Kip's looking at Matti like in some horribly mushy movie.

No! They cannot ride off together into the sunset, ignore me, break up, and become enemies then make me to choose who to be friends with. That'd be as easy as deciding whether to cut off my left leg or my right.

I get between them. Fast. "What was that?"

"What was what?" Matti says, straightening herself out and fumbling with her backpack.

"Since when do you trip and fall?"

"Since my backpack strap came loose and got tangled in my legs." She holds up the backpack. "Good as new."

But even Kip's looking at her funny like he doesn't believe her. And when we ride home, I can exhale only when he turns toward his street and Matti doesn't follow him.

An hour later things still feel weird. I break my grounding rules and call Matti. "What's going on between you and Kip?" I ask. It's so much easier to be blunt without those big brown eyes of hers making me feel even shorter than I am.

"I thought you were grounded from the phone."

"I think you're stalling." I take the cordless to the front window to watch for my parents. It's almost five thirty.

"I don't understand your question," she says.

"What's not to understand? Are you and Kip going out?" There. I said it.

"Going out?" She practically howls with laughter. "Going out?" she says, a little too loud. "Going out?" She's protesting too much. "Travis. I am not going out with Kip. That would be like going out with my brother."

"But you like your brother."

"And I like Kip. And I like you. And I like puppies. And I like hot fudge. And the only two of the above that have any chance of touching my lips are puppies and hot fudge," she says. "And where in the world would you get such a stupid idea?"

"You mean, like when one of the most coordinated people I know—"

"Thank you."

"Trips and lands in a hug with my other best friend? Then you give him this look—"

"Like I appreciated he didn't let me fall flat on my face and break my nose?"

"Well, it didn't look that way to me."

My mom's car turns into our driveway. Followed by my dad's.

"Gotta go," I say.

As I run to put the phone away, I picture her face again, and I know she's either delusional or lying. Something's going on between the two of them.

I can't do anything about Kip and Matti now, but I can look inside the envelope.

I go to my room so my parents don't suspect I've been doing anything besides homework. Curry follows me. I start to close my door, but I open it again because I normally keep it open until they get home, and I don't need to add my parents to the list of people watching me even more closely than ever.

I sit on the floor with my bed as a backrest, and Curry curls up and uses my leg as a headrest. I grab a notebook and pencil and pretend I'm writing something.

Both my parents come in to say hi and to thank me for following the rules, and I really don't feel bad because I was only on the phone with Matti for a minute. Besides, it was urgent. If I hadn't talked to her, I wouldn't be able to concentrate on anything tonight.

When they go downstairs to make dinner, I dump the coin out of the envelope and put it with the other two. I stick out my tongue at the unexplainable math sequence still in my drawer. Then I pull out the new puzzle paper, which make my eyes jumpy.

Place these items in a plain, white envelope. Deposit the envelope in the office attendance box by the end of school on Wednesday.

What items? "Just looks like a bunch of blobs and lines to me, Curry." I hold the paper up to her face, but I'm afraid if she licks it, the lines will turn into smears and I'll have less than zero chance of solving what must be a puzzle here.

Idea! I pull out the other paper I got today. Maybe it's a clue for this puzzle.

You are about to enter greatness. The secrets are about to be revealed. Follow the directions exactly and you will become one of us.
The Legend of Lauer

I stare at it for five minutes, but there's no clue here. Maybe this is just encouragement. Keep your nose clean, Travis, and you'll be rewarded.

I look back at my lines. Idea. They look like a bar code. What if I scan it at the store and it tells me to bring in a package of cookies? The attendance lady would like that. Not so much if it's for vinegar. But what if it's not a bar code and I waste a trip to the store? And an excuse to get there. I need to check the pantry.

I head downstairs, and the sound of TV drifts from the den. I miss that sound. I tiptoe toward it, taking a huge step over the part of the floor that creaks, hoping both my mom and dad are in the kitchen making dinner. I get on my knees and scoot across the wood floor until I can see half the TV screen over the back of the couch, without parents' heads.

It's nothing I want to see—the news—but it's TV. I stay behind the couch and watch for about five minutes before Curry notices me. She scampers over, and my mom's head pops up, apparently from its lying-down position.

Busted!

"I was coming down to get something," I say, "but then I stopped to hear the interesting story about identity theft."

Her face says she doesn't believe me, but she finds me amusing, even when she grills me about calling Matti. I can't believe she checked redial on the phone. But I don't get annoyed, partly because I am guilty as charged and mostly because she's not mad after I tell her it was important.

I take no punishment as a prize, go look at bar codes in the pantry, and decide they're too different from my puzzle. I have no other ideas now, so I stay and help my dad with dinner. After we eat, my parents banish me to my room, which is fine. I zigzag up the stairs, knowing the puzzle will stare at me until I figure it out. And I will. Otherwise the paper wins. And a kid should be able to beat a piece of paper any day.

I plant my feet on the hall floor just outside my room, pull the door mostly shut and grab the doorknob. I lean in and the opening door pulls me into the room, diagonally. I let go, flop onto the floor, and drag myself to the bed like a guy in a desert crawling toward an oasis.

Except a page with skinny lines is not an oasis.

I lift myself enough so my hands can grasp the top side of my bed. I let my arms hoist me up until I'm eye level with the bed's surface and the puzzle paper. And I'm a genius. At least I think I'm a genius.

From this angle the lines have gotten shorter! The lines have turned into letters!

And right now I have only one question. Why am I giving them seven nails?

CHAPTER
■ 17 ■

It's no problem they're asking for seven nails, like it's no problem they asked for an *i* and a trash can. But it's all so random. If they want random . . .

I put seven nails into the envelope and laugh. These are not the nails they're expecting. I return the fingernail clippers to my parents' bathroom.

The next morning I deposit the plain, white envelope into the office attendance box. I picture the attendance lady getting really grossed out, and that keeps me smiling until science, when I really start grinning. We get to work on our worm farms.

The worms have migrated to the second tray, and we

need to harvest the fertilizer they've made. We take out the first tray, and a few worms are still in there.

"Eew!" That comes from a few people. We've been doing this all year, so you'd think they'd get used to a few slimy worms. It's not like they bite.

I pick one up and move it to the second tray. So does this girl Sari, who didn't eew. "I think we should name them," she says.

"But how would we tell them apart?"

"If you name one Curly, you can call, 'Hey, Curly,' and whichever one looks up, well, that's Curly." She's so smart, we know she's not serious. I wonder if she's in The Legend.

I wonder if everyone in The Legend is so smart. Or if they all look alike, like these worms or like plain, unmarked envelopes. I stop grinning. How will The Legend people know that particular envelope is from me? Should I have put my name inside? Will the attendance lady know where to deliver it? And what if she gets so grossed out that—

"Travis!" Sari's looking at me in horror.

"What?"

She points to my hand. "You're—"

I'm squishing a worm. I toss it into a tray. "I didn't mean it. I didn't do it that hard. I didn't kill it or anything. I . . ."

I decide to shut up.

"What happened?" says one kid.

Randall the oaf snickers. "He just pulled a minor Travis this time."

"A minor Travis?" I say after school. "A minor Travis?"

Kip and Matti look at each other, which bothers me in more ways than one.

"My name is now a synonym for stupid, boneheaded mess-up? Who started it? When?"

Kip raises his chin toward the oaf. "They started it on Friday."

I pound my fist into my glove. "You've known since Friday?" I say to Kip.

He can't look right at me. "I thought it would go away like everything does around here."

"So far nothing has."

Matti steps up to Kip. "He's not blaming you," she says. I'm glad she can still read my mind. Or maybe she's reading his. "He's just upset at the world. You should know that by now."

"I just don't like to be blindsided by anything," I say to Kip.

"No one does," he says. "Sorry."

I hate that I upset Kip. It's bad enough that my name will become a dictionary definition. Travis: see *stupid*.

But I'm not stupid. I wish I could announce how I solved four impossible puzzles. No, three and three quarters. I still don't know why that one number is 23.

Pulling a Travis. At least Kip and Matti've heard it only from oafs. At least no one dares say it when we're at baseball. They know I don't mess up on the field.

Why can't I learn to be that Travis inside school? Why did I put fingernails into the envelope instead of hammer-and-nail nails? What if that's enough to keep me out?

I hurry to my hall locker after the game—which we lose—hoping to find something positive so I don't have to worry I messed up again. There's a normal blue envelope.

All right. But why are there always eyes around? I put the envelope into my backpack, then Kip and Matti and I get our bikes and pedal out of here. Kip turns toward his house, Matti turns toward hers, and I turn down the next street, pedal for about ten seconds and stop my bike under a big tree. No one's gonna bother a kid looking at a note.

If you want to be part of The Legend at Lauer, follow all our instructions exactly.
Rule #1. Don't chew gum unless you have enough to

share with the whole class.

Rule #2. 6th grade lunch. 11:30 Friday. There must be enough gum in the cafeteria to share with the whole class.

Rule #3. Don't get caught.

The Legend of Lauer

They want me to buy gum for everyone in sixth grade? Not for my friends? Since when does The Legend single out one grade? Maybe always. Maybe I never really paid attention. Fine. Anything for The Legend.

So how many people in sixth grade? And how much does gum cost? How much do I have in the train bank on my desk?

I get back on my bike and speed to the grocery store. I don't have a cent in my backpack, but I can find out how much I'll need.

I run to the candy aisle, grab the biggest pack of bubble gum . . . and wow. I'll need more than the seven dollars I have left from the birthday money I got from Grams and Gramps, the not-dead grandparents. I never should've bought that lame video game all the oafs were going nuts over. Showed me not to listen to oafs.

I want that money back plus half the money I caught in

the money booths, especially because I didn't win the signed Chase Maclin guitar. It felt good to be generous, and The Legend basically made it impossible not to be, but still.

I get back on my bike and pedal harder and harder because there's something weird about this. If The Legend had all that money to give to the food bank, and if they sent ten kids and their parents to the Olympics the year before, then why are they expecting a kid like me to use a hunk of his own money to buy bubble gum for the sixth grade? Wouldn't they at least shove a twenty dollar bill into the envelope?

But that's not my only question. I feel another one about to erupt.

There's the money thing and . . . what? What feels weird?

Okay. They had me spend money on the trash can, right? No. I bought the trash can, but I could've drawn a picture of one for the cost of a scrap of paper and a smudge of pencil.

That's not it. What am I missing?

I'm missing a puzzle. And a coin. And I'm missing the answer to this question: are all the envelopes really from The Legend?

CHAPTER
▪ 18 ▪

It's Wednesday and five minutes before lunch, my social studies teacher, Mr. Huff, hands me a note. No one knows what it says except me and him, but when I pick up my backpack and head to the door, it's a non-oaf who says, "Did he pull another Travis?"

I want to punch the guy in the face, but I grin and raise an eyebrow. I can't let them see how much this all bothers me: his comment and the summons to Mrs. Pinchon's office.

I don't know what she can accuse me of unless I have an evil twin or I went temporarily insane. I knock on her door, and before she waves me in, I notice her face from behind her desk: she's not gonna name me King of Lauer today. "We meet again, Mr. Raines."

My neck's usually not in knots when principals call me in. It's happened so much, I must be immune. But with The Legend and soccer captain and soccer camp, I have too much that could disappear before I take my next breath.

"I need to ask," she says, "if you know anything about three gallons of hand soap missing from the janitorial closet."

"I didn't take it. I swear."

She spins the chain of her mirror-ball necklace like she's trying to hypnotize me into telling the truth. "No one is accusing you, Travis. And you're not the only one I'm asking."

"So, you're rounding up all the usual suspects?" I mean it seriously, but it suddenly sounds ridiculous. I try to hold back my smile.

She smiles at me, though. "It's okay. That was humorous."

The buzzer sounds. Time for lunch.

Time for Mrs. Pinchon to stiffen back up. "Still," she says, the smile wiped off her face, "whatever's going on here is serious. Be on notice that whoever is messing with this school—and those who may be protecting them—will be punished. Fully. Is that clear, Mr. Raines?"

"Yes, ma'am." I stop myself from kicking open her door. She said she wasn't accusing me, but I'm the only one she called from my class. She didn't draw my name at random.

I grab my lunch bag from my locker and stomp down the stairs. I turn toward the cafeteria, and there in the library hall is the oaf. Mrs. Pinchon should be talking to him.

My first instinct is to go kick him in the shins, but instead I'll walk to lunch and leave his big face buried in his locker. But it's not his locker. It's the 207 locker hall. And Mr. McKenzie said no one has lockers down here.

I stop. I see him see me. And I see what he shoves back into that locker.

A shine-under-the-surface blue envelope.

Randall's getting blue envelopes? Or is he giving them? Punking me. Either way they can't be from The Legend. An oaf like him isn't smart enough. He is evil enough to set up a whole fake Legend thing and force some smarter oafs to write the puzzles. Then they'll all gather around, watch me make a fool of myself, and laugh hysterically at the end of his oafish joke.

Gotcha, Randall. Gotcha where you've been stashing my blue envelopes.

I head straight toward him. "What are you doing here?" I say.

"What?"

"What are you doing here?" I say oaf-slow, also trying to get a look inside the locker.

He slams it shut. "Whatever I want."

Typical. "This isn't your locker. No one has lockers down this hall."

"Maybe I do now." He clamps the lock shut and gives the numbers a twirl.

"Fine. Lock it. But I know the combination."

He gives me that dopey stare.

I need him to give me answers. "Talk to me about envelopes."

"Envelopes?" He gives the lock another turn. A hard turn. "You put letters in them and mail 'em out. That's all I know." Good thing he doesn't lie for the CIA.

I look at him like he's toast. "What about the next envelope?"

"There's no next envelope in the locker."

He is so dumb. "I didn't say anything about any envelope being in the locker."

"Shove it," he says, but he doesn't shove me. His eyes, though, look for a place to settle. And that place is starting to look like a dent in my head. One he wants to make.

I can't make him mad, not before he takes away my evidence. "What if I tell you something I know, and you tell me something back?"

"Why should I tell you anything when you go around accusing me of everything?"

"What'd I ever accuse you of that you didn't do?"

"Forget it," he says. "Just leave me alone. The whole group of you."

I can't lose him before he spills something. "I'll prove I know about the envelopes. If I can't open that lock on the first try, you can pummel me."

He takes half a step aside.

I move in and spin the combination wheel right to 32, left to 23, then right to 16. I tug.

He grabs my hand.

"Don't touch me."

"Don't open the locker." He lets go but blocks the door with his whole hulk.

"Afraid I'll get proof of what you and your little double-oh-seven wannabes are doing to me? 'For your eyes only'? Ha!" I smash my fist into the locker next to him.

The library door flies open, and Mr. Drummond juts his head out. "I know you have somewhere else to be. Get to the cafeteria, and keep the noise down."

Normally I'd love a teacher to break up any contact with Randall Denvie. Not now. I need to get into that locker, but more than that I need to stay out of trouble.

I catch up to him and match his stride till just inside the cafeteria doors. That's when I cut him off and steer him to the puke green cinder block wall. "Don't bother denying it," I say. "I saw the envelope."

"Big whoop. Should we alert the media?"

"Good idea. Let's haul it out and show the world what you're doing."

"No!" He whisper-yells with enough hot air that I can smell his before-lunch breath. Onion-breath would be better.

"Then admit you have a shine-under-the-surface blue envelope with my name on it."

His eyes shift left then right. He backs off. "It doesn't have your name. It has mine."

His name? He's getting puzzles and coins? But he's an oaf. He has to be lying. "So, this is your first one, right?" I say, testing him.

"Do you just have one?"

Now he's testing me, but we won't get anywhere unless I say something. "More. You?"

"That was my fifth."

He got five? Why'd I put fingernails in the envelope? I stare at him. He grins back at me like we've been chosen for the same team.

Problem is I don't want to be on the same team with him. It's bad enough he's in science and Spanish and sports with me in seventh grade, at Lauer Middle School, on Earth.

I push away from the wall. "I'm going to eat."

I look up. My lunch table is staring at me. Not the table itself. My friends at the table. I'd be staring if I watched me have a no-yelling conversation with Randall Denvie.

"I hope you're not getting friendly with the enemy," says Kip even before I sit.

"Not exactly," I say.

Seven pairs of eyes keep staring, waiting for an answer.

I need to scramble for some excellent excuse. If we're both getting envelopes, I have a feeling this won't be the last time they see me and Randall talking. "It's complicated."

"It's not so complicated," says Matti, getting right to the point. "What'd he say to you? What'd you say to him?"

"It was nothing," I say. "I ran into him in the hall, he

started yelling at me, then Mr. Drummond told us to take it to the cafeteria." I shrug, then I smile. I told the truth. Sort of.

My smile shrivels. They know there has to be more. I take a bite of my Swiss cheese and mustard sandwich, and chew and chew and chew and chew until it's so mushy I have to swallow.

They're still waiting.

And so am I. I'm waiting for inspiration. And Ms. Skrive, my English teacher, passes by and gives it to me. Blame it on an adult.

"I was in Mrs. Pinchon's office," I say, the right words leaping into my brain.

"Again?" Matti says.

"I wasn't really in trouble." I tell them about the soap.

"Did you take it?" asks Katie.

"Are you nuts?" Matti says. "Travis is the most honest person I know."

Great. This story I'm about to tell is a total lie, but at least it's a lie that won't hurt anyone. "So I sort of accused Randall of setting me up. And Mrs. Pinchon said maybe Randall won't bother us if we're nicer to him. Maybe he's acting out of jealousy."

I have no clue where this psychological stuff came from. Maybe bully episodes of ancient TV sitcoms. But I go with the story and say I was making the first move.

"Obviously it didn't go too well," says Matti.

"I promised Mrs. Pinchon I'd try more than once." I roll my eyes for effect.

"Well, that stinks," says Katie.

Everyone agrees except Matti. "Why is it that teachers don't hate him? Pretend I'm a teacher. Tell me why he's such a mean oaf. Give me ammunition."

She's nuts.

"You're nuts," says Kip. "You know it all, Matti. But if it'll make you happy, there's last year when Randall shoved Marco's soccer ball underneath Mrs. Bloom's car so she'd run it over."

"Then why did I see Marco the next day kicking the same ball?" She is nuts.

"What about Jackie Muggs in fourth grade?" I ask. "Randall sent him to the hospital. Almost dead. Thirty-eight stitches."

"Did anyone see it happen?" she asks.

Kip's turn. "There was the cupcake incident in second grade."

Mine. "And breaking Natalie Levin's leg last year. And basically crippling mine for the rest of the soccer season two years ago."

Matti shakes her head. "Those could've been accidents."

"Not the worm farm," I say. "He deliberately knocked my arm so the worm-and-dirt tray crashed to the ground, which got me in such deep trouble, I had to skip soccer practice. And my five dollars and eighty-five cents from fifth grade. And hey," I say. "What about Kip's cap?"

"I heard he didn't do it," says Matti. "Not on purpose at least."

"Then why didn't he fight back when Marco said he did?"

Matti unleashes her hair from her ponytail. "I don't know."

"Then why are you sticking up for him?" I say.

"I'm not." She gathers her hair back behind her. "Call it a momentary lapse into Teacherland. Forget it."

I can't because Mrs. Pinchon's voice is echoing in my head. *Things aren't always as they appear.*

Randall is sitting a few tables over with Marco and four other oaf types. He looks at me, and I jerk away, knocking over Katie's giant water bottle.

Kip and Katie and the rest jump around getting napkins and trying not to get wet.

Matti nudges me. "What's this really about?"

I pretend I don't hear her. I'd rather say nothing than lie directly to her. I join the mop-up crew and switch the topic to soccer camp. Katie tells me about this new drill she found online, and I have her show me. People stare because we're really good at pretending we're kicking the ball and guarding each other.

And I'm about to ask if anyone has a ball so we can kick it around during our five-minute recess when I catch Matti and Kip trading a weird look. Matti mouths a word to Kip. Kip shrugs. Then she pushes him like the time Natalie pushed me in first grade when she liked me.

"Okay," I say. "What's going on?" I look directly at Matti then Kip.

"Nothing," he says. He couldn't lie for the CIA either.

The rest of the day plummets from there. Not that anything bad happens, just that I get called out for not paying attention and stuff. But how can I concentrate on school? Soccer camp and soccer captain may be running away. I may have to lose one of my best friends. I'm getting all these instructions. I'm not so happy about paying money for gum to give to sixth graders. And I feel like I'm about to get in trouble for that, but I'm not sure how.

So I think I'd like to drop out of life and move to Monrovia for a month then come back and figure everything out. By then, though, I could lose out on becoming part of The Legend. At least I still have the promise of that.

Problem is so does Randall.

CHAPTER
▪19▪

I spend most of Spanish getting whiplash, turning away every time Randall glances at me. He even smiles once, which is totally creepy.

Do I really want to be in The Legend if he's in it, too? Stupid thought. I'd pay every cent I ever had to get in. Even for bubble gum.

I get home and nearly wipe out my train bank, seal the money in an envelope, stash it in my backpack, ready to dash to the store after baseball tomorrow. Alone.

Before practice I tell Coach and Matti and Kip I have a doctor's appointment and skip out two minutes early. I buy the gum, bring it home, and then I check the school phone book, which I forgot to do last night. "Curry, I could've bought three bags less."

I should start my homework, but I spread the ten packages of gum around me and stare. What do I do with it? Throw pieces around the cafeteria so it looks like a gum factory exploded? Dump whole bags at the cafeteria doors? Hand it out as the sixth graders come to lunch?

No, no, and no. In the first case, a cafeteria adult would clean it up before anyone gets a piece. In the second, someone would hog all the bags. In the third, I'd be totally exposed.

I try to ignore my stomach, which is rippling like the time in soccer when I took the pass from Katie, dribbled the ball downfield, and shot the winning score with thirty seconds left in the game. But not. This isn't nervous excitement. It's more like something's wrong. Something more than figuring out the gum delivery system. I think my gut's telling me I'm getting two sets of instructions.

Questions attack my brain like nails to a magnet.

Question: Why would they suddenly start signing their instructions from The Legend? Answer: In case we're getting frustrated, we know, for sure, it's worth it.

Question: Why are there two different kinds of envelopes? Answer: They don't have enough of the shiny kind. Answer number two: They use different kinds for different reasons.

Question: Why would The Legend want to include anyone like the oaf? Answer: They wouldn't. The shiny envelopes aren't from The Legend. Answer number two: Things aren't always as they appear, and Randall just appears to be an oaf.

Question: If they're from two groups, which envelopes are real? Answer: No answer.

Question: If they're both from The Legend, what happens if I don't do everything they ask? Answer: I wouldn't be that stupid. End of questions.

What's the harm in being the Gum Fairy? The sixth graders'll love it. Besides, The Legend's special because it's sneaky and surprising. I mean, who'd predict they'd pick me to—

Blump-blump.

"Come in," I say automatically.

My dad looks down at me sitting inside the semicircle of packages. He doesn't say anything. Just raises his right eyebrow.

"It's something I have to do for school."

"Right," he says. "You have to build Bubblegum Mountain."

"It's not like that."

"Travis. I've heard that line before."

How can I prove it without breaking— "Wait. You signed a permission slip with a mess of rules. Or mom did when you were in Japan. It's part of that."

"Okay," he says, "but where did you get all that gum?"

"I robbed a bank." I show him my almost-empty train bank.

My dad opens his mouth to say something but closes it before any words come out. This can't be good.

He goes out the door, and without looking back he says, "I came in to tell you it's dinnertime." He turns toward his bedroom.

I don't follow him. Maybe he needs time to get unangry about whatever he thinks I did. I go to the kitchen, but he's only five seconds behind me.

He hands me a twenty dollar bill.

I should take it and say thank you then nothing else, but I forget to make sure my mouth's in on that plan. "What's this for?"

"Yeah," says my mom. "What's that for?"

"For Travis going above and beyond and taking responsibility." He tells my mom about the gum then gives me extra points for being secretive and following about four more rules.

He gushes so much, I hate to tell him the money doesn't quite cover the cost of the gum. I didn't expect a cent, so it's all bonus. But I'd rather trade it for a way to dump the bubble gum. Which, after dinner, is staring at me so much I can't do my homework.

I stash it all into two grocery bags, but then I stare at those. I've gotta get out of here. I go downstairs and hear my mom in the kitchen.

She has the oil, flour, and sugar out and is reaching for the measuring cups. I go into the freezer where we store the poppy seeds.

"While you're there," she says, "get out the eggs and a lemon."

"A lemon? Moon cookies aren't lemony."

"Maybe not, but there's another taste we keep missing, so I thought I'd try lemon juice."

I understand the point in trying stuff, especially now with the puzzles and gum and everything. I put the eggs and lemon on the counter and open the cabinet to get the salt and baking powder. "These cookies are like a great big puzzle to you, aren't they?"

"There's that, but there's more." She measures out the

flour. "My mother made moon cookies. My grandmother made moon cookies. My great-grandmother made moon cookies, and who knows how far back it goes. If we stop trying, who else will keep the recipe alive?" She dumps the flour into the mixing bowl. "There are some traditions worth preserving. What better than cookies?"

What better? The Legend.

I know what to do with the bubble gum.

CHAPTER

■20■

I run upstairs and write a message on notebook paper. Then I shred it.

After naming me King of Responsibility at dinner, my parents have to let me on the computer. "I promise," I say to my mom. She's cutting out the cookie circles. "It'll take me five minutes. Ten at the most. And it's for school."

Thirty seconds later I'm on the computer. Within five minutes I'm printing what I need.

I think about finding some fun websites real fast, but if being good gave me twenty dollars and a few minutes on the computer unsupervised, I can wait five days, when my two weeks are up.

I put the printed paper into the gum bag and head to the kitchen. "I need to borrow the tape," I say to my dad, who's in the den. "I'll bring it back after school tomorrow."

"Done with the computer already?"

"Yep!"

"That's my boy!"

Those good feelings keep me calm all night, but I squirm so much in my chair during English, Ms. Skrive comes up and whisper-asks if I need to use the bathroom. What does she think I am? Three years old and just out of diapers?

I have four more minutes before I need to get this bubble gum drop started. Maybe it's a good thing I keep squirming because by the time I claim the bathroom pass, I think Ms. Skrive is relieved I didn't, well, relieve myself in class. I throw the cord of the pass around my neck and speed walk to my locker where—score!—there's a new, shiny envelope.

It's too complicated to deal with two sets of instructions at once, so I grab only the plastic grocery bags that have the gum, the roll of tape, and the printed sheet of paper. I take off the bathroom pass and shove it inside my knee pocket, then pull out the hall pass Mrs. Pinchon gave me on toilet paper flood day when

I was late for lunch. If anyone stops me and studies it hard enough to see that the time and date are wrong, I'll figure something out.

I look at the clock down the hall. Six minutes until the bell rings for sixth grade lunch.

Perfect. If I get there too early, some teacher or other adult'll find the gum before the kids do. If I get there too late, some kid'll see me put the gum there.

It's Friday Lunch Shuffle, and the table assignments are posted on every cafeteria door. That means kids will actually read signs there. I dump the individual bags of bubble gum out of their plastic grocery bags so they're blocking one of the doors. Then I tape my sign next to the table assignments.

IT'S LEGEND GUM DAY!
To the first person who finds the gum by the door:
It's your responsibility to make sure every 6th grader gets a piece of gum at lunch. If you do not follow these instructions, you might get banned from every Legend Event forever. Figure out a way to make this happen, and we will remember you helped carry on our tradition.
BECOME LEGENDARY!

If that doesn't work, nothing will. I stuff the tape into my pocket and the grocery bags into the trash can and pick up speed to get out of there before the bell rings. I take a right, head halfway up the nearest staircase, and bump straight into Mr. McKenzie. "Sorry," I say.

"Back at you," he says, but then he points down the stairs. "The cafeteria's that way."

"I have to—"

"Wait. You're in seventh grade."

I flash the old pass at him, and before I pull it down, he swipes it from my hand and dangles it over his head.

"I'm thinking if I look at this, something will be fishy."

"I swear, Mr. McKenzie," I say, "I'm where I'm supposed to be, but I will get into trouble if I'm not back in class before the bell rings. Three minutes."

He doesn't move for eighty-three years, then he lowers the pass. "Be good."

"I will." I race up the stairs, down the hall, and get this shiver down my neck, feeling a little guilty about the lying, and also about using The Legend name in my note, but none of it's for evil. Thirty more seconds and I'll be back in class and—

Er-er-er! Er-er-er!

Fire alarm! Where am I? Where's the nearest exit? That way.

I push open the door, shove the old hall pass into my pocket, hang the bathroom pass around my neck, and find my class outside.

I breathe in. No fire smell. I try again. Nothing. False alarm.

The good news: everyone's safe. The bad news: Johnny Flood's in trouble again.

It takes only fifteen minutes before they figure out it was a prank. It'll take longer than that to clear my name.

When my next class lets out, every voice in my head yells at me to go straight to the cafeteria and blend in, but my legs move me to Mrs. Pinchon's door. I knock on the glass.

"Don't tell me," she says before I get all the way inside. "You were passing the fire alarm and your shirt got caught on it, wouldn't let go, and accidentally pulled the lever."

"No. I'm here because you'd call me in anyway, and I didn't want to go through the humiliation of being pulled out of class. I also came to remind you that things aren't always as they appear, and that I didn't do it, even though I had the opportunity."

She rests her chin on the points of her fingers. "You had the opportunity?"

I nod. "I had the bathroom pass, so I wasn't in class when the alarm went off."

"And who's your teacher?"

"Ms. Skrive."

"The same Ms. Skrive whose classroom is not near the second floor bathroom where Mr. McKenzie saw you? Travis," she says, "they know which alarm was pulled."

I slump into her chair and shake my head. "Just because I didn't go to the nearest bathroom doesn't mean I did it. If I did, would I be here? Besides, why would I do it when I know I'd get kicked out of life the next time I did something bad? I may not be as smart as a lot of people, but I'm not stupid either."

Mrs. Pinchon ekes out a piece of a smile. "No. You're definitely not stupid."

At least that's something. Now if she'd only quit staring at me.

"Before I excuse you," she says, finally glancing away, "I'm curious. Do you know anything about bubble gum in the cafeteria?"

Uh-oh. What would a normal kid say? "There's bubble gum for lunch?"

"No." She twirls her mirror ball. "Someone claiming to be from The Legend brought in gum for the sixth graders. Though, with the fire alarm, it wasn't all handed out."

Not my fault, but I can't worry about that now. I need to worry about my next normal-kid line. "Someone from The Legend? Who?"

"It doesn't matter who."

I smile. "That's okay. I'll find out at lunch."

"Which, you'll also find, is mostly in the gym for you seventh graders. We need to give the sixth graders time to buy and eat their lunches," she says, putting on a very serious face. "And you know what that means, don't you, Mr. Raines?"

I shake my head.

"We'll need to pay the janitorial staff overtime to get all the crumbs and grease and sticky jelly bits off the gym floor."

I think about Mr. McKenzie and his expensive car and the extra money he'll get from the overtime. And the missing soap. And him snitching on me being in that part of the building.

Did he pull the fire alarm? And if he did, why would he want to frame me?

CHAPTER
▪21▪

I'm walking with Matti and Kip to the bicycle rack after school, and they're wondering why we don't practice on Fridays, when we have two extra days to do homework.

I keep my mouth closed. If I open it, I'll blab about bubble gum and fire alarms and blue envelopes. I want to tell them everything. They're the ones who kept me sane when I misheard my dad's phone conversation and thought we were moving to Australia. They were my alibis when someone put Whiskers the rabbit in the gym. They always have my back. But they won't have it unless I tell them what's going on. And I can't.

I can complain about Mr. McKenzie without spilling

anything. "Why is he always around when I get into trouble?"

"Think about it, Travis," says Matti. "You do seem to cover every part of the school in the course of the day. And the halls are his turf."

"But it's a big school," I say. "Why can't he catch me doing something good?"

Kip and Matti both look at me.

"Okay, okay."

"Besides the fire alarm and the toilet paper," says Kip, "he hasn't caught you."

"He wasn't around when you went up on the roof," Matti says. "He didn't see us lock you inside your locker last year. He didn't blame you for the marble incident."

"What marble incident?"

"This morning? The bucket of marbles rigged to dump all over the gym? Coach Ford finding it before it spilled? How did you not hear?"

I lean over to unlock my bike. "Probably because I didn't get blamed."

"Exactly," she says. "Mr. McKenzie didn't blame you."

I shake my head. "Still, he seems to be all around me ever since—"

"Ever since what?" Kip asks.

My first blue envelope? Can't say that. "Ever since I went onto the roof."

"Maybe," he says, "Mrs. Pinchon asked him to watch you."

We pedal off, and I wonder if the assistant principal in charge of discipline really did assign a janitor to watch out for me. I can't be that bad. I'm still getting envelopes.

I ride home, sling my bike into the garage, grab some dog treats for Curry, fill her water bowl, and sit in the living room to open my envelope. My parents won't be here for a while.

First, there's a blue note paper clipped to the bigger sheet of paper.

LOL, Travis! Bodily nails! Bravo!

Bravo? All right! Let me at this next puzzle.

If May 7 July 19 = eggs, then
February 21 March 11 May 20 =

Please slip a representative underneath the teachers' lounge door by the beginning of school on Tuesday.

Here we go again. Brain freeze. It's gonna get stuck on eggs and calendars, and they probably aren't part of the answer. But what if they are this time?

I start with eggs. What do I know about them? Birds, reptiles, and amphibians lay them. So do fish. Mammals have them but not like you'd normally think. People put them in cakes and other dessert stuff. And I don't love them all that much except for those chocolate and marshmallow ones I've had at Kip's, which taste light years better than last night's moon cookies. Too lemony.

I grab the cordless and call Kip. "Isn't this the chocolate egg time of year?"

"Yeah. Come over if you want."

"Uh . . ."

"Oh," he says. "You're not even supposed to be on the phone, are you?"

"Yeah. See you on Monday."

Fine. Back to the puzzle. I move my mind from eggs to the calendar and check ours to see if the dates on the puzzle are holidays. Nope. The closest is February 21, which could be Presidents' Day some year. The others could be made-up holidays like National Kiss Your Elbow Day or Balance a Lucky Penny on Your Head Day, but that'd be stretching things.

So I have nothing but a worthless calendar in one hand, a nonsense puzzle in the other, a fourth coin ready for my drawer, and a blue envelope on my lap. I take a tenth look inside the envelope to make sure I didn't miss anything. I didn't. And—

Curry starts barking, runs to the door, and the bell rings. Doggie ESP.

I stand on my toes to look out the peephole. Kip! I open the door.

"Delivery," he says through the screen part. He holds up a plastic baggie with four of those candy eggs in it.

"You're the best!"

He reaches to open the screen, and I do, too, until I realize what's in my hand. I quick-shove the blue envelope and the coin behind the window curtains next to me. Not that Kip would recognize them, but I don't need anything else complicating my life. And I don't want to lie to the friend who would pick up and come over with four chocolate eggs.

So I especially don't want him to see the puzzle on the couch. I steer him to the kitchen and we both devour an egg then go out to kick the soccer ball and talk about soccer camp and how afterward he's going to basketball camp while I do nothing the rest of the summer. And pretty soon the next-door neighbor's car pulls in. Ricky and Charlie, who are about three and five, spring out the door and start chasing our ball. Sort of an on-the-ground keep away.

Mrs. Barron opens the trunk and pulls out some groceries. "Ricky! Charlie! Leave those poor boys alone."

"It's okay," I call back. "Okay with you, Kip?"

"Yeah," he says. "This is actually more fun."

"If you don't mind watching them, I'll be right out once I've put these away. Yell if you need me before that."

By the time she comes back, we've pretty much ditched the ball, and we're rolling in the dirt, all five of us: Curry, too. Probably not what a mom wants to see, but she laughs. "I guess it's bath time," she says. "C'mon, boys!"

"We wanna play wif Travis and the big boy some more," Ricky says.

Mrs. Barron comes and takes them each by the hand and walks them toward their house. "Travis will play with you again tomorrow."

I will?

"He's helping us dig in the dirt and plant our new flowers."

I am?

She turns back and smiles at me. "About ten in the morning?" she calls.

"Sure," I say, wondering when I agreed to that.

Ten minutes after Kip leaves, my mom gets home. I hear her but stay in my room and pin the puzzle to my dartboard over the ugly picture of Randall, the one from the sixth grade yearbook I blew up at the copy center the day after he kicked a soccer ball into my nose.

I throw my first dart. It hits below the writing. I aim the . . .

Am I stupid? What if I totally decimate the puzzle and never get it solved? What if there's a secret code in the fiber of the paper and I ruin it?

Okay. I doubt that. Still. Mistake. I take off the paper and look at it again until my mom calls me downstairs.

"What have you been doing?" she asks. She points to the little rug that sits inside the back door from the kitchen.

"Wiping my feet?"

"Looks like you wiped ten people's feet."

Just two people's, I'd say if I wouldn't get into trouble. Kip came in and ate six moon cookies. He liked the lemon. "I was rolling in the mud with Ricky and Charlie," I say. "And I think maybe someone here volunteered me for something and didn't tell me about it."

"Oh yeah." My mom pulls the lettuce from the

refrigerator. "I thought you'd rather help Mr. Barron plant flowers and bushes instead of doing my boring chores."

"You might have asked me first."

"Yes, and you might have asked me before you hung over the edge of the roof."

"Aren't I still paying for it?"

"Exactly."

I shake my head and give her a smile. A nasty one, though, and she knows it. "I think I'll keep quiet and set the table."

"I think that's a good idea." She tears into the lettuce, tosses pieces into the salad spinner, then pushes the spin button extra hard before she looks up. "What's the deal, Travis?" she asks. "On any normal day you would have celebrated if I arranged for you to play in the dirt."

I don't want to talk about any of it, but that's suicide around here.

"It's nothing," I say, getting out three napkins. "I got blamed for other things I didn't do."

"What?"

"Someone pulled the fire alarm when I wasn't in class. I had the bathroom pass."

"And you didn't do it?" she asks.

"You know I wouldn't."

"You wouldn't." She takes a piece of chicken from the bowl and shakes off the extra marinade. "What else? You said, 'other things.'"

I tell her about the toilet paper and the soap, and I'm surprised Mrs. Pinchon never alerted her. Maybe there's hope. Maybe Mrs. Pinchon believes me. Either that or she believes I'm totally guilty and wants me to get overconfident so she can catch me once and for all.

When I finish, my mom looks straight at me and I feel even smaller than my puny self. "Honest, Mom. I didn't do any of it. I don't do mean stuff."

She almost nods. "You may get into trouble, but you've always had a conscience. You've never done anything malicious."

I should feel better, but she's still looking at me.

"Here's the problem," she finally says. "You've put yourself into a position where people believe you're capable of masterminding everything that goes wrong. You can't have a happy future that way, Travis. You have to change."

She turns on the stove and puts the grill pan on the flame. And she doesn't lump on any more punishment. At least not any real punishment. I walk upstairs to my room, and those words about the future feel worse than getting grounded.

How can I make everything right? Maybe I should've asked my mom, but I didn't and I know why. This recent trouble started with the envelopes. If I ignore them, the trouble will stop.

But no way I'm ignoring any envelope.

CHAPTER
▪22▪

After dinner I decide there's only one thing to do. Fast-forward through the puzzles.

If May 7 July 19 = eggs, then
February 21 March 11 May 20 =

I need to forget eggs and calendars. They're not part of the answer, like hats and crackers had nothing to do with the second puzzle.

That puzzle was pure weirdness at first, but the weirdness helped me solve it. So, what's weird about this one? For starters, no punctuation between the dates. That has to mean something. So does the reason they chose those dates.

That's all I have except legs that need to move. So I knee-jump on my bed. May 7 July 19. May 7 July 19. Two months, two dates. Two and two equals four. Kip brought over four eggs. Four letters in the word "eggs." Eggs. Eggs. Should I eat the last two eggs? I bounce higher. Harder. I do not need more sugar, not after brownies for dessert. Okay. The puzzle. May 7 July 19. May 7 July 19. Four eggs. Four letters.

I stop. Why am I suddenly obsessed with the number four? Two dates. Two pieces to each date. One answer. Four letters. Idea! But can it really be this easy? I write myself a key.

A	B	C	D	E	F	G	H	I	J	K	L	M
1	2	3	4	5	6	7	8	9	10	11	12	13

N	O	P	Q	R	S	T	U	V	W	X	Y	Z
14	15	16	17	18	19	20	21	22	23	24	25	26

May's the fifth month, and the fifth letter is *E*. May what? May 7. Seven equals *G*. July's the seventh month. G again! And nineteen? EGGS!

Let's do this. February's the second month. *B*'s the second letter. Letter 21? *U*. March 11. *C*. *K*. May 20. *E*. *T*. Now, what can I slide underneath the teacher's lounge door besides a boring picture of a bucket?

I keep wondering while I'm digging at the Barrons' house. I could tape a handle onto a collapsed origami cup—we made those in fourth grade—but I don't remember how to fold one, and the computer's still off-limits. I could draw a picture of a deer with big antlers, then a plus sign, then a first-aid kit like one of those rebuses—buck + kit—but my deer would probably look like a puddle attached to some plankton.

By the time Charlie comes to help me dig, I'm sort of resigned to the fact that I'll have to draw a bucket good enough that they don't mistake it for a purse.

With Charlie the digging's going slower, but I guess it's okay because Mr. Barron thanks me for letting him help. So, there's Charlie in one part of my mind and the bucket in the other. And when I get home, I pull out my mom's old copy of *Charlie and the Chocolate Factory*, and I'm right. The kid's last name is Bucket.

I tape the book jacket to the window, tape a piece of plain paper over it, and trace the thing with a pencil, including the title, the little Willy Wonka guy, and what

I'm hoping are Charlie's eyes. I might not be a good drawer, but I'm a good tracer. And so they understand what I'm thinking, I draw a red arrow pointing to the kid's eyes. At the end of the arrow I write, *His last name.* Then I put the paper into my backpack.

I'm at school on Monday right when the doors open. I slide the tracing into the teachers' lounge with no eyes around. None at all.

By lunchtime I haven't gotten into any trouble either. Not even little trouble as in "Travis, are you paying attention?" trouble. Then Katie and Matti keep cracking jokes, and I almost blow milk through my nose. And I'm feeling really good, going to my locker to grab books for my afternoon classes. Then I see a regular blue envelope. Even better! Any envelope gets me closer to the end. I duck into a bathroom stall.

Travis,
The principals think you pulled the fire alarm, which should be enough to kick you out. But without proof, we're giving you another chance. Dig up two of those yellow flowers you planted yesterday and put them back in their pots, which we saved from the trash and which

are on the side of your house. Put one pot outside of Mrs.
Pinchon's door and one outside of Principal Wilkins's
door with a note that says you're sorry. Tomorrow
before school.
The Legend of Lauer

I kick the toilet seat. It flies up and crashes down. I unlatch the door and kick it open.

I can't dig up those flowers. I can't. It's not that I spent four hours over there planting them. I just don't steal. Period.

CHAPTER
▪23▪

I don't hear anything my teachers say the rest of the day. I strike out every time I'm up at bat. I drop two routine pop flies in the outfield. I apologize to Coach and Matti and Kip and whoever else is listening at the end of the game. Then I pedal my bike out of there like a madman, trying to figure out how to steal flowers without getting caught. Or if I should even try.

Why would I want to be in a group that asks me to do something so wrong? But The Legend isn't. The Legend tries to make things right. That's why those seven kids started—

My brain kicks into overdrive. My legs stop pumping quite so hard. That's it!

The website! How The Legend started! Kids doing things wrong for all the right reasons. The note asked me to do something right, but in a wrong way. This has to be a sort of puzzle. An extra test to see if I can figure out the right way to apologize even though I didn't do anything wrong.

I ride straight to the Barrons' and knock on their door.

Ricky and Charlie are yelling my name from the other side. Mrs. Barron opens up, and the boys push past her and beg me to play soccer again. If I can stop panting long enough to ask my question then get the answer I need, I'll do anything.

I make my neck work overtime and look Mrs. Barron in the eye. "I can't tell you why," I say between breaths, "but how mad would you be if I dug up two of your yellow flowers today if I promise to replace them with my own money as soon as my mom or dad can take me back to the store where you bought them?"

She gives me that what-are-you-talking-about look they must teach all parents. "I suppose it's okay, Travis," she says finally.

"Thank you so much," I say. "I promise I'm not doing anything wrong. I'm trying to do everything right, and that's why I'm asking."

"Just be careful not to tear the roots when you're digging."

"I will. And do they want to help?" I point to Ricky and Charlie.

The boys jump up and down, grabbing onto my legs, and I'm feeling really good about everything. Especially about figuring a way out of this mess.

My parents agree to drive me to school early in the morning then drive me back home so I can ride my bike. "It's that thing," I say, clutching two plants and two apology notes.

They smile at each other. My dad says he'll buy the flowers as long as I put them back into the ground myself. My mom drops them off at school for me.

Because I didn't get into trouble over the bubble gum or the flowers, I get this vision of The Legend people sitting around their secret location wondering why they didn't induct me into the Legend Hall of Fame when I was three years old. I knocked this one out of the park.

So I go through the second day this week without getting into trouble. Better still, I get rewarded with a shiny blue envelope at my locker.

I go home, drop my fifth coin into my drawer, and get to work solving the puzzle.

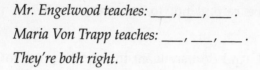

Mr. Engelwood teaches: ___, ___, ___ .
Maria Von Trapp teaches: ___, ___, ___ .
They're both right.

v e v e e e   e v e e

Tack a representative onto the music room bulletin board by 5:00 P.M. Thursday.

Okay. So, Mr. Engelwood teaches sixth-grade band, seventh-grade band, and eighth-grade band. I've never had him because when I tried the trumpet in fifth grade, the thing sounded like a dying hyena and I didn't want to stick around a roomful of other dying animals to see if we could get better.

But who's this Von Trapp lady? What does she teach? I open last year's yearbook but don't see her anywhere. Her name sounds familiar, though, like my mom might know her. I reach for the cordless but stop. Rule #4 says I can ask questions that sound like homework help, but I never call for homework questions. I usually use the computer.

It's Tuesday! I call my mom. "I can use the computer right? It's for school."

"I was under the assumption your punishment ends tomorrow. Is it urgent?"

"Never mind," I say. Or maybe I groan it.

I hate following the rules, except the ones that make sense. And I have to admit that most of The Legend rules do make sense. Except for #6.

Remember, when opportunity closes a window, it often opens a door.

A window? A door? Why can't it be an Engelwood and a Von Trapp?

I guess it's supposed to be inspirational, but it doesn't inspire me to solve the puzzle. Maybe my old toy keyboard will. I find it in the basement.

I remember enough about reading music because of the posters in the elementary school music room. One had notes—F, A, C, and E—in the spaces, and the notes had faces. The next poster's notes looked like cabbages, and they spelled CABBAGE.

What if the notes spell out my next thing? I write out letter-notes.

DDFCEDACBE

It was worth a try. So's picking out the tune on the keyboard, but the song doesn't sound like any song I've ever heard, not even by the time I'm back upstairs humming it from memory. I need to know something about Maria Von Trapp before I can solve this puzzle, but what if I find out about her and still can't solve it?

I've solved every one so far, haven't I? Unless you count not understanding 23 from the math sequence sheet. It's still in my underwear drawer and it taunts me every day when I get out my briefs.

51, 32, <u>23</u>, 14, 25, 16, 17, 18

I swear I hear it even now. "Nah-nah-nah-nah-nah-nah! You can't figure me out. You might not figure out the next puzzle either. You don't know what this Envelope Madness is all about, and there's no one you can ask, is there?"

There is. His big oaf smirk flashes before my eyes then stays in my brain. What if Randall figured out the sequence? That'd make me stupider than an oaf.

I start an extra-credit math sheet. Hah! Number

sequences. Just looking at them sends a microscopic slug crawling under my fingernail, inching its way up my arm, winding over my shoulder, up to my ears, taunting me even more.

I look up Randall's phone number, and before my brain can stop my hand, I punch it in.

"You know that locker combination?" I say after we trade minor insults.

"I know lots of locker combinations."

Why'd I bother calling? I should've let that slug crawl under my skin. "Look," I say.

"At what? We're on the telephone so I can't see what you're seeing."

"Randall! Isn't it possible you might need blue-envelope help in the future?" I exhale. Loudly. "I have one stinkin' question about one stinkin' number sequence."

Silence.

"It starts fifty-one, thirty-two, then the blank, which I got. But why's it twenty-three?"

"You don't know?"

"Would I call if I did?" I say. "I just want an explanation. Can you give me one or not?"

"Not without proof."

"Of what?"

"You saw one of my envelopes. I wanna see one of yours. And the math sheet."

"Fine," I say. "Stay right there."

For once I'm glad Randall lives close. I wasn't when we carpooled to soccer for four years. But it's 5:13, and I need to be home by 5:30. In case I'm late, I record a message and put my tape recorder on my parents' bed. Then I ride my bike with my backpack weighing down my shoulders. I should've pulled out my books first.

I ring the bell, but the oaf won't let me inside without an envelope and the math sheet. I dig them out, flash them like a secret code, then slip the math sheet back into the envelope.

He cracks open the door and reaches his hand out. "Lemme see."

I hold the envelope closer. He snatches it and lets the screen door slam. While he's inspecting the string clasp and the For Your Eyes Only ink stamp, I fling my backpack off the porch, behind some bushes. I don't need his grubby hands to snatch that, too, just to annoy me.

He opens the door wide enough to let me in. I try not to gawk at the inside of his house. I expected a bed of nails and other torture chamber devices, but there's an antique table with a fringed lamp and a soft couch with an old-fashioned quilt. And his mom. I forgot he had one.

Randall walks me straight to her. "Mom, you remember Travis Raines. Travis, you remember my mother, Janice Denvie."

What kind of weird alternate universe have I entered? She gives me the nicest smile and comes to shake my hand.

I hold mine out and give hers the type of firm handshake my dad taught me. I remember to look her in the eye. And I can. She's short. Size-wise, there's hope for me yet. Or maybe Randall's parents adopted him from some giganto mutants.

Randall leads me upstairs.

"Are you adopted or something?" I ask his back.

"No," he says from the top step. "My mom's from Alabama. They're polite down there."

"I don't mean that." I pull even with him. "She's short."

"So are you." He leans his forearm on my shoulder.

I duck under and make him go off balance. Serves him right.

We go into his room. Or his shrine. We step over his St. Louis Rams rug and past his display of signed footballs.

He tosses my envelope onto his dresser and lowers his oafness onto his Rams bedspread, perfectly spread. If his whole room looks like it jumped from a sports museum, why'd he toss Kip's cap instead of swiping it for his collection?

It's 5:20. I have seven minutes. "Let's just do this," I say, leaning against his dresser.

"I don't know if I should," he says. "You got rules, didn't you?"

"There's nothing in the rules about explanations after we figure out the answer."

"Then how'd you get the answer?"

I explain.

"Cool." He tosses up a Nerf football. "So why do you think we're doing this?"

It's 5:22. "I have an idea," I say, "but telling you might be against the rules."

He shrugs like he's buying it. "I guess we'll know soon enough. Do you think we'll beat Russert Middle School next game?"

"Baseball?"

"No, Candy Land."

I smile even though it's Randall and even though it's 5:23.

He tosses me the football. Sort of soft. I toss it back, and he holds on to it. "I heard you might be soccer captain next year. That's cool."

And you're the reason I might not. But I don't say that. No reason to provoke the enemy in his own territory. "Gotta keep myself out of trouble." I give him a look to remind him it's all his fault, but he's not looking at me. "You going to soccer camp this summer?" I ask, hoping his nice mom will ship him off to some nice island instead.

"Nope," says Randall. "No more soccer. It's all football all the time starting in summer."

We toss the football back and forth and back and forth until I hold on to it. "Randall," I say, "if I don't leave here in three minutes, my mom'll kill me for being late. She's not from Alabama, but she has her rules, too." I toss the ball back.

"Yeah," he says. "I've been thinking. If I tell you, you need to give me something."

"Like Kip's cap?"

"You've got that all wrong."

"You're not the one who took it off my desk?"

"Yeah, I took it off your desk, but . . . Never mind."

5:25. "Right. What do you want?"

"An insurance policy. If I need help, you give it to me."

"But I didn't need help."

"I just want a hint for a hint." He soft sails the ball into the mini basketball net hanging on his door. "I might not even collect."

That's what worries me. Maybe he's also smarter than me. 5:26. I make the deal and pull the number sequence from the envelope.

51, 32, _23_, 14, 25, 16, 17, 18

"Look at it," he says. "Look at the second digit of each number."

"I already told you they go in order. So what's with the first digit?"

He rolls his eyes. "Of all the digits in this problem, how many are ones?"

I count. "Five."

"Very good. Now," he says like a parent talking to a two-year-old, "how many twos?"

"I get it. Fifty-one means five ones in the sequence, thirty-two means three twos then two threes, one four, and yeah." I never would've figured that by myself.

Who thinks I'm that smart? Only my parents, but they're not giving Randall blue envelopes. "Thanks," I say, getting ready to be civilized for his mom again. But I'm not feeling as uncivil anymore. I point to his football signed by old running back Marshall Faulk. "Cool."

"Yeah," he says. "I actually met him once."

"Cool," I say again, and head for the door.

Randall blocks it. "I need to walk you out. Manners and all."

My shoulders stand at attention again, ready to fight. "Then why aren't we walking?"

"Maybe I want that hint now."

He goes around me, grabs a blue envelope from his desk, then teases a blank piece of paper in and out. "Did you get this one yet? Did you figure it out?"

I want to see if there's something on the non-blank side, but I also need to get out of here. "Even if I did, you don't want to waste your hint yet, do you?"

He thinks for a second.

5:27. "You know where to get me," I say, more confidently than I feel. "I'm outta here."

I can make it home in three minutes. I fly down the stairs, Randall sticking behind me. He opens the door for me and I'm out. I climb over the porch rail and jump to the ground next to my backpack, lean over to grab it and—

Really? I sit and pretend to tie my shoe, but I'm looking in the gap under the porch. I'm looking at three-gallon containers of school hand soap.

CHAPTER
▪24▪

"I hate Randall Denvie," I say to Matti as we're walking to lunch, my first chance to talk to her today.

"What else is new?"

I tell her about the soap.

"Did you ask him why it's there?"

I look at her like she's nuts. "We both know why it's there. He stole it and has been laughing ever since they blamed me."

"You weren't the only one they blamed."

"Still, if he doesn't swipe it, Mrs. Pinchon doesn't accuse me. So I hate Randall Denvie."

We get to our table and Matti spreads the news for me.

I don't want to talk about it anymore. I want to slug the nose off that guy's face.

I almost went back there right away and did it, but he deserves more than a black eye.

I look over at him, and he looks at me and lifts his fingers off the table, almost like he's waving. I give him a stare that would freeze tongue-blistering pizza in ten seconds. He comes back with a stare that would freeze it in five.

I lower my head in Matti and Kip's direction. "We need to rat him out without the oafs knowing it's us. After baseball? I'm un-grounded."

For the first time in forever, or two weeks, we ride to Kip's after practice. Used to be, I'd pull peanut butter and graham crackers from his pantry, but Matti beats me there and grabs marshmallow fluff and chocolate chips with the grahams. "Quick s'mores," she says. "I made it up when you were in detention and they were out of peanut butter."

I should've known Matti came here without me. I watch her open all the right drawers and cabinets while Kip feeds his cat. It's almost like they're married. If they start touching, I'll scream. Unless I puke first.

Thankfully they don't hold hands or nudge each other.

They don't even sit on the same side of the table. Matti sits with me.

"You're absolutely positive," she says, "that it's the school's soap and not theirs."

"Same brand. And parents would store it in a garage or basement, not under a porch."

"I wonder why he didn't hide it in his room," Kip says.

"His room's perfect," I say. "A speck of dust couldn't hide in there."

Kip gawks at me. "You were in his room?"

Matti slugs me on the shoulder. "You were grounded, and you went to his house but not here or to mine?"

How do I get out of this one? "It's a boring story," I start, hoping I can come up with any story. "I needed homework help." Sounds good. "And if I sneaked over here and my mom found out, I'd still be grounded." Even better. "But going to Randall's is actually more punishment than staying home, and well . . . I'm not grounded anymore, am I?"

"And you made it out alive!" says Kip.

"But I'll be re-grounded and dead if I don't get home by five-thirty." I point to the clock. It's 4:24. "So, how do we get Randall?"

Kip turns to Matti. "This is your department. You're the one with the good ideas."

Thank you, Kip.

"What if we send an anonymous note to Mrs. Pinchon?" she says.

I shake my head. "Straight-on tattling. Anyway, what fun is that, Matti?"

"I didn't know this was supposed to provide our minimum daily requirement of hilarity."

"It's not," says Kip. "For once we want Randall to get caught, in public."

"Exactly. Caught. Tarred. Feathered. Completely humiliated."

"No," says Kip. "Somewhat humiliated."

"No stripping him naked in the middle of the cafeteria?" I take a bite of my fake s'more and push my chair back. "Get your soccer ball. I can't think when I'm sitting."

We take it outside and kick it around. We rule out hiring one of those planes to fly a banner around. Or putting up a billboard. Or hijacking the school announcement system.

"What if we tell the TV news to film the soap so we have evidence?" Matti says.

Kip kicks the ball to me. "That's sorta like the idea we

already rejected about making a reality TV show out of it."

"No. It's not," I say. "Evidence. That's what we need. We need to take a picture of it. Maybe a close-up. Then one a little farther away. Then farther and farther until you can recognize his house and see the street address. Then we post the pictures at school."

"That's genius, Trav," Kip says.

Matti shakes her head. "It's almost genius, but there's a problem."

"What problem?"

"Suppose someone did that to you and you felt cornered."

"Okay," I say. "We'll think of something else."

"What?" Kip says. "What's wrong?"

"Doesn't matter if I stole the soap or not," I say. "I would yell and scream that someone played a bad prank on me and they planted the soap to make me look bad."

Kip nods. "That leads to another problem, doesn't it?"

"What?"

"What if someone did plant the soap to make Randall look bad?"

"If someone did," I say, "they'd have ratted him out already."

We decide to take pictures, print them out, shove them

under Mrs. Pinchon's door, then let her figure out what they mean. It's almost tattling, and it's not exactly fun, but we have nothing else.

One problem. How do we sneak up to Randall's front porch and take the pictures when no one's looking? Correction. How do I sneak up? I've been elected.

CHAPTER
■ 25 ■

Only one person can take the pictures, and three's a crowd. Besides, it's my problem. Like everything else.

I want to get this over with, so I jump on my bike and they don't stop me. By the time I get home to grab the camera, I'm not sure it's a good idea. It's still snitching, I could get caught, plus it doesn't feel right. If I change my mind, I can always do it tomorrow. Today I can use the computer! I can look up Maria Von Trapp from the puzzle.

Curry settles next to the desk. She's crunching her biscuits and I'm hitting the keys, and it's a great combination of noises.

What's not great, according to the Lauer website, is that there's no one named Maria Von Trapp in the entire school district. I'm hoping for just a few hits when I type her name into a search engine, and . . . overload!

This'll take forever. Or not. Maria's from the movie! *The Sound of Music.* Matti always played the DVD at her house when we were little. "I mean, younger, Curry. I'm still little."

And Maria taught those Von Trapp kids to sing. "Teaching music, Curry. That's what Maria and Mr. Engelwood have in common."

> *Mr. Engelwood teaches:* ___, ___, ___ .
> *Maria Von Trapp teaches:* ___, ___, ___ .
> *They're both right.*

If they're both right, it has to mean they do things differently. How does Mr. Engelwood do things? Katie'd know. She plays the French horn, but I can't exactly ask her about Mr. Engelwood and Maria Von Trapp without telling her why.

Now what? I pace down the hall. Curry follows me. I pace back. Curry must think I'm nuts, but I am remembering. When Maria teaches the kids, they sing that famous song. That do-re-mi song.

Do, re, mi! She teaches the do-re-mi way! Mr. Engelwood must teach music the A-B-C way like we learned in elementary school. Exactly what I tried before.

On a clean piece of paper, I match the note-letters and the do-re-mi ones.

A   B   C   D   E   F   G
dough ray me   fa   so   la   tea

Is that right? No. No way do they spell dough like moon cookie dough. There is doe like the deer in the song, but why do I think it's spelled D-O, which looks like do as in, "Do you really think you can rat out Randall without being killed?"

Maybe not, but I can finish this puzzle.

I love the Internet! The musical scale doesn't even start with A. Now, it is right:

C   D   E   F   G   A   B
do   re   mi   fa   sol   la   ti

So if I'm supposed to use *A-B-C* sometimes and use do-re-mi other times, how do I know when to use them? I guess I take one note at a time then try all the combinations, guaranteeing to make my brain hurt. Or . . .

Why didn't I notice those in the first place? The little *v*s and *e*s. And if *v* equals Von Trapp and *e* equals Engelwood, I can spare my brain. I give it a try.

First note. D with a little *v* for Von Trapp. I write *re*. D with a little *e* equals *d*. F, little *v*: fa. Three little *e*s. CED. And if the rest mark is a space, I have "redfaced." I think that's a word. Four more notes. A C B E with a little *e* then *v* then *e* and *e* which translates to A then DO then B then E A. DO. B. E. Redfaced adobe. Redfaced adobe?

"What's that, Curry? Like adobe houses in the Southwest?" I open the dictionary again. *Adobe.* "They're bricks, Curry. Redfaced bricks. Red bricks. Like the ones on our house. Or the ones on Randall's attached to the porch near the soap."

Oh yeah.

CHAPTER
▪26▪

5:18. Do I have enough time? Not if I stand here. I snatch my parents' digital camera from the computer desk drawer, and for the second day in a row, I'm racing like a madman, a different madman than yesterday. Yesterday I was mad at myself for going to Randall's to get answers. Today I'm a madman on wheels, taking the corners like an Olympian, pedaling like my legs are superpowered. But I can't exactly tear across his lawn, jump off my bike, let it clatter down, jump to the side of his porch, and start clicking the camera.

I lay my bike on the lawn next door and pray no one swipes it, then fly up the far side of the neighbor's house, race through the backyard, and surface at the back of Randall's. I hunch below window level and move between the brick and the bushes. Five feet from the porch steps, I drop flat to my belly and pull the camera from my knee side pocket. I hit the power button.

Buh-lee-duh-lee-dit!

The power-up noise is loud as a doorbell. Quick: I zoom in on the soap, hold still, shoot. *Kah-chee!*

Zoom back. Soap and porch steps. *Kah-chee!*

Scoot back. Soap, porch steps, and brick. *Kah-chee!*

Get on my knees and—

"What are you doing?" Randall's towering over me from the top of the porch.

"I . . . I . . ." I hold up the camera. "Found it! I dropped my backpack when I left yesterday, and it fell out." I point the camera at Randall. "Let's see if it still works."

Kah-chee!

I zoom it back so I can get him and the porch steps. *Kah-chee!*

"I'll be going now," I say.

He's standing there, glaring at me. He's gotta be wondering if I saw the soap and deciding if he should slug me and get the camera.

I want to run, but he'd catch up to me. Maybe not

tonight but tomorrow. Idea. I press a button. "Hey. Good picture of you. Look!" I hold up the camera so he can see it's him and not the soap. I turn it back around and pull up the second picture of him. "This'd be better if you smiled, but you can see it if you want."

He glares some more.

C'mon, Randall. Take my bait. I wouldn't show you the pictures if I had something to hide, would I?

He comes down the steps. "Lemme see that first one again," he says.

"Fine, but look fast. I have about two minutes to get home." I show him.

He narrows his eyes at me. "What's before that?"

Do I bolt? No, I smile. As long as I don't give him the camera . . .

"I don't know what's here," I say. "Probably some stuff my parents took." I go forward, not back, praying the camera still has old pictures like always.

Great. Well, it's better than the alternative. It's me doing a cannonball into a hotel swimming pool a few weeks ago. Then my mom lying on one of those lounge chairs. He does not need to study my mom in her swimming suit. I turn the camera screen away from his eyes.

"What are those from?"

"Spring break. My dad had business in Costa Rica and we went with him. Frequent flyer miles and all." Why am I telling him more than he needs to know? "I need to go."

"Then go."

I slide the camera into my pocket and take off to get my bike.

"Why's your bike way over there?" he says, hanging off the porch.

"Got the wrong house at first then didn't bother to move it. See ya," I say.

Randall doesn't stop me.

I pull into my driveway three seconds before my mom does.

"Cutting it close again, Travis?"

"Yeah," I say. More than she knows.

While she's making dinner, I download the pictures of Randall and the soap, print out two copies of each—one for delivery and one to keep—then delete them from the computer and the camera.

I fold one set, seal them in an envelope, and put the envelope into my backpack, all ready for tomorrow. But they're not going under Mrs. Pinchon's door. The pictures have bricks. Redfaced adobe. I'll nail the envelope to the music room board, then sit and watch The Legend nail Randall.

CHAPTER
▪27▪

I jolt out of bed long before my alarm goes off, run to the computer, find a website where they sell bricks, and print out a picture.

I almost made a huge mistake. Disastrous. If the Representative Collector shows the pictures to Mrs. Pinchon, who shows them to Randall, he'll know where they came from. I'll be dead within the week. I put the sealed envelope into my desk, just in case, then send the other pictures through the shredder. I'll figure out Plan B later.

I get to school just as the doors open. Almost no one comes this early. I run upstairs before any other eyes can, and I stick the new brick picture on the music room bulletin board. I remembered my own tack.

Matti and Kip won't be here yet, so I go the long way to my locker, past the front offices.

Bad idea.

Mrs. Pinchon and Mr. McKenzie are standing in the middle of the hall, staring at me with a look that'd make a monster run the other way. I force my feet to keep walking.

Mrs. Pinchon turns to Mr. McKenzie. I think she says, "I'll take it from here, Ralph."

He walks off but looks back at me before he turns the corner.

Mrs. Pinchon plants her hands on her hips and raises her question-mark eyebrows into those red bangs. "A word, Mr. Raines."

I follow her into her office.

"Sit," she says. That's all. That's bad.

I sit as still as my body will let me.

She towers over me. Her hands are folded together except for her two index fingers, which are pressed together and sticking straight up. She bounces them against her lips. Finally she takes a deep breath and her hands come away from her mouth. "How are you doing this?" she says. "Why are you doing this?" This must be bad. She's not yelling.

My heart races. "Honest. I don't know what you mean."

She nods. "Then why are you here so early this morning?"

"I woke up at five and couldn't sleep because I realized I did an assignment wrong, so I did it right, and I didn't have anything else to do besides come to school. Then you saw me, and I think I'm in trouble again, but really, Mrs. Pinchon, I didn't do anything wrong."

She stares.

"What do you think I did?" I say. "And how can I prove I didn't?"

She goes around her desk and sits. "First there was the toilet paper. You had opportunity. Then there was the soap. Opportunity again. Fire alarm. Opportunity. And now today. Opportunity. Our mops, brooms, and buckets are missing."

I shake my head. "I don't like to mop floors," I say, but the humor doesn't work. I should stick with the facts. "I didn't have opportunity. I left home just a few minutes ago, and I was home all last night after baseball. Call my parents and—"

"Brringk- brringk!"

Mrs. Pinchon answers her phone. All she says after that are "hmm"s and "I see"s. My life as I know it probably depends on what the person at the other end is saying.

She hangs up. "Exactly what time did you get here this morning?"

"Five minutes before you saw me. Maybe less. I promise."

She does that bouncing thing with her fingers and lips again. "You'll find out anyway," she says. "A couple of our swimmers found a broom jammed into the pool's filter and a bucket at the bottom. The rest are still missing."

"I wasn't anywhere near the pool. I was near the music room."

"You don't take music, Travis."

"I know, but I stopped because of something on the music room bulletin board."

"And that was . . . ?"

"An ad for bricks. I was curious why someone would want to sell bricks to people in the music room. So I looked at it."

Mrs. Pinchon gets on the phone and waits for whoever's at the other end to check for my ad.

It'd be simple if I could tell her I'm doing this for The Legend. I mean, I should be able to. My parents know about it, but according to Mrs. Bloom, not all the teachers do. What if saying something bans me forever? And why would I steal mops and stuff? Why would—

Mr. McKenzie! If he couldn't do his job during normal hours, he'd get overtime pay tonight. But accusing him would just make me look desperate.

Mrs. Pinchon hangs up. She narrows her eyes like Randall did yesterday. "No bricks," she says.

They took it away already. "Maybe Mr. Engelwood took it down. Maybe he saw it and knew it didn't belong there."

"That was Mr. Engelwood on the phone."

Perfect. "What can I say to prove I'm innocent? I mean, you saw how surprised I looked when you accused me. I'm not that good an actor. Besides, why would I make up an ad about bricks? That's too random to be a lie, isn't it?"

"You have a point."

"And I'm not a bad person."

She whips her head toward the window and coughs. "No, I don't believe you are." She clears her throat and looks back at me. "However, Mr. Raines. Until we straighten this out, you are not to be in this school before seven thirty in the morning. After school you are not to be in this building except for necessary time in the boys' locker room. That means you bring everything you need to your practice, for your protection and ours. Now I suggest you stop lurking in the hallways and this morning go straight to class. Math class, I believe."

"I need to stop at my locker first. Is that okay?"

"Go."

I feel so lucky, I don't even get mad about missing before-school time with my friends. I promise myself I'll get my stuff, sit in my math room, and barely breathe.

Before I open my locker, I can see the normal blue envelope through the vent. I take it into the deserted math room.

Saturday, 7 A.M. Go to the back stairs outside school. Find the bundle with your last initial. Pick it up. Put 5 bottles of syrup where the bundle was. Follow the directions in your bundle. Don't mess up.
The Legend of Lauer

CHAPTER
■28■

Do they think I try to mess up? Did they forget the original Legend people messed up? I am not messing up anymore. They didn't ask for a representative, which means I'm buying ... syrup?

Maybe The Legend's bringing in the famous Pancake Lady from last year. But they never repeat anything. Can they repeat Rule #5 to my parents, though? That I have to do secret stuff? Rule #5 should help when I tell them I'm taking syrup to school on Saturday morning, which wouldn't be a problem if I skipped the fact that I got accused of stealing mops and brooms and buckets. But I'll tell them.

Hey, I might as well tell everyone. So, when word gets out, I admit I was questioned. I smile when people call me Johnny Flood and laugh when others say I pulled another Travis.

I don't fool Kip and Matti, though. When they ask about the brooms, I refuse to talk. I've never done that before. I need to figure out how to explain why I've been lurking around school, which is impossible without telling them about blue envelopes.

I don't wait for them after practice. I go home, take Curry out to do her business, bring her back in, and leave the door open while I fill her bowls. Then I watch for them from the living room window. After they realize I left school without them, they'll come here to find out why, unless they're sick of my problems. Maybe they won't come.

I go back outside to get the mail. No Matti, no Kip, but no mistaking the blue shining from underneath the magazines. The envelope doesn't have a stamp or a return address. Someone dropped this off today. My lungs deflate. I'm out. I know it. I stand just inside the door, unwind the string, peek in the envelope, and yes! I can breathe. It's another puzzle! Not a nasty—

"Where'd you go?" Matti's voice says.

I pull the envelope to my chest.

She looks at it. Stiffens. Looks at me. At the ground. "Kip's coming, too," she says.

My first instinct is to shuffle the envelope with the mail, but I don't bother. It's obvious she recognizes it. "What?" I say, waggling it the air.

"Cool envelope," she says.

Fine. We'll play it that way. I shove the envelope under the couch cushion as Kip comes in. "Food, anyone?" I say.

"Sure, but look out, will you, Kip?" She pushes past him and heads to the kitchen.

"Real nice, Matti." I close the front door. "What's with her?" I say to Kip.

He shrugs, and we go into the kitchen, where Matti's already moving stuff around in the pantry.

"Help yourself," I say.

She moves more stuff. "You got any soda?"

"You know we do." I go into the small fridge in the laundry area, pull out three cans, and when I come back, Matti and Kip are standing in the pantry too close together.

Two minutes ago I would've worried that they were together. Not now. Not with her whispers, which turns into loud whispers. I catch a few words. "But Kip . . . blue envelope."

That's enough. I clunk the soda cans on the counter. "You have something to tell me?"

"No," says Kip. "Matti's hallucinating."

If she knows something, then forget all the rules. "Are there blue envelopes in your hallucinations, Matti?"

She looks at me like I slapped her in the face.

Kip quick-studies his fingernails.

I take a chance, go into the other room, bring the envelope back, and wave it all around. "Does this mean something to you?" I point directly to the words FOR YOUR EYES ONLY.

Matti looks at Kip, who's darting his eyes like he's scoping out an escape route.

"It has to mean something to you, Matti. You're not talking."

"I don't know what it means, okay?" she says. "Anyone can buy blue envelopes. I've seen them at Walgreens or Spicer's or somewhere." She looks back at Kip.

He shakes his head.

"Just leave it alone, Trav," she says. "Just let it play itself out, okay?"

"Okay." I open a can of soda. "No. Not okay. I need

to ask you a question. Did both of you know about the money booths last week?"

"Huh?" says Kip.

"Let me be more clear. Are both of you in The Legend?"

Matti grabs a box in the pantry. Macaroni. "Why would you say that?"

I just stare at her.

She hides her mouth with the box. "They don't tell us who's coming in."

Kip's freckles stand out. "She did not say that." He shakes his head. "And if it is The Legend, it's probably secret anyway. I hear they have rules."

"Have you seen some rules?" says Matti.

"If I have?"

"Rules are rules," she says.

"Yeah, but since when do you play by the rules, Matti?"

Her eyes become snake slits. "You know I don't cheat."

I look right back at her. "Not in games and not in sports, but you're just like me, Matti. Sometimes the rules suck and these rules suck. They're part of the reason I'm getting into trouble. So when rules suck, Matti, we push them a little. That's the truth."

She doesn't back away. "Truth, Travis? The truth is this looks like The Legend and smells like The Legend, but The Legend doesn't get people into trouble. The Legend isn't—"

"Matti!" Kip pulls her arm.

She drops the macaroni. "I'm not breaking any rules. I'm not saying I know what The Legend is. I'm only saying what it isn't." She puts the macaroni away and pulls out a box of chocolate-covered grahams. "Maybe it's best if Kip and I pretend we didn't see anything."

"Okay," I say. "We can pretend. But I have a problem. I follow directions, I get into trouble. Why is that?"

Kip's sitting at the kitchen table staring at his fingers.

Matti opens the cookies then sits, too. "Did you ever consider," she says, "that maybe someone's setting you up? Not The Legend. Maybe some person who has something against you. And he's waiting until you're all alone then doing stuff to get you into trouble? It's not like you don't have your enemies."

"Yeah, but watching me seems like a lot of work." I join them both at the table. "So, if people already know where I'm supposed to be and when, it'd be easier for them to frame me, wouldn't it?"

Kip slumps. "You can't be accusing us."

"No, Kip. No way. But I'm getting weird instructions and doing what they say and—"

Matti's grabs my fingertips. "It was you. Your fingernails."

Kip even smiles for a second. "Look," he says. "I know it's hard, but believe me. Blue-type instructions will not get you into trouble if you keep following them."

"And from here on out," Matti says, "we will always have your back."

I want to understand this completely. "So, you know about Saturday and where I'm supposed to be and when I'm supposed to be there and what I'm supposed to do and why I'm supposed to do it?"

Kip nods. "And like Matti said, we've got your back. Now, can we just leave it alone and eat cookies?"

CHAPTER
▪29▪

After they leave, I can't stop jumping up and down. They're in The Legend! They've been all secretive because they're in The Legend. They're not boyfriend/girlfriend. And they have my back.

What they don't have is a way to clear my name. I have to do that myself.

I pull my sixth coin and a blank piece of paper from the blue envelope. Maybe like the puzzle from Randall's house? Paper clipped to it, a normal blue envelope contains a paintbrush and a picture of a grape juice bottle.

So, I'm supposed to paint with grape juice on this

piece of paper and what? Deliver it to the art room? And what am I supposed to paint? A crayon? An eggplant? More grape juice?

I go to the computer, and because I can, I type into the search engine: *grape juice paintbrush paper*

Oh yeah! I run downstairs. "Do we have any grape juice, Mom?"

"You don't like grape juice."

"Maybe I do now."

She gives me that look.

"Okay. It's for school. Like a science experiment."

"Invisible ink?"

"How'd you know?"

"I was a kid once. Call Dad and ask him to get some on his way home."

I rush him when he gets here, and he hands me the grape juice and also the five bottles of syrup. "This is getting expensive," he says. "I hope you're almost done."

"I do, too," I say, but knowing about Matti and Kip has given me a second wind.

I set up my grape juice art studio in the bathroom, dip the brush into the bottle, and— Wait. What if this isn't invisible ink? What if I ruin the puzzle?

I smile and brush the grape juice. If I mess up, Matti

and Kip have my back. Hoo-hah! I won't need them. I keep painting the paper and make the disappearing ink reappear.

Put a handle on the desk
in Room 207 tomorrow.

Is a doorknob a handle? I have an old, broken one stashed under my bed. I learned you can't swing like a monkey holding both knobs of a bedroom door without breaking something no matter how small you are. Dictionary time. *Doorknob*. Bingo! Knob-shaped handle!

Problem. How do I deliver it after seven thirty without eyes? I need a shield. I call Matti. "You really have my back?" I ask.

"You know I do."

"Will you stand guard while I make a delivery tomorrow?"

"You know I will."

I coordinate it so I meet her and Kip a few blocks from school, and we cruise to the bicycle rack together. I lead them into the building, up the stairs, and down the hall. They wait while I go into Room 207 and dump the broken doorknob onto the math teacher's desk. Mission accomplished, with witnesses I didn't need.

I'm almost sorry nothing bad happens all day. But I do get my parents' permission for Saturday morning as long as I take a cell phone and call them every minute. Rule #5 rules!

I can't get to sleep Friday night, and I wake up at 4:48 A.M. Saturday morning. I squirm in bed until I can't stand it anymore. I get dressed, eat breakfast, and finally, at 6:47, wake my parents to tell them good-bye.

It's eerie riding your bike soon after sunrise. The light outlines the tops of everything—houses, trees, utility poles—but below, it's all murky, like my brain feels now.

It works enough to understand I can't park my bike in an empty rack if I need to stay invisible. Besides, it's so spooky quiet, I want it with me. I'm glad I have the phone. I'm glad I have the syrup in my backpack, too. I could wonk someone with it if I had to.

I cruise up the school driveway then stop to speed-dial home and say I'm here. I wheel my bike onto the grass, veering toward the back of the school where there's not much looming except creepy trees and spooky silence.

I'd be more scared, but Matti and Kip said they knew

where I'm supposed to be and when and why. And don't secret societies like The Legend always make things extra mysterious before they let you in? So I try to get excited. This is it! The end! No more puzzles, no more envelopes, no more creeping around!

It's not working. The more I try to get excited, the more my knees feel like rusted metal. I force them to keep moving toward the outside stairwell that leads to the basement. The more I do that, the louder my bicycle wheels and feet *shush* over the grass. Like each step's saying, "Go back, Travis. Go back."

I spin around. Look behind me. I'm not going back. This is all good. Matti and Kip and the other Legend people'll jump out at any minute and celebrate with me.

Closer. Closer. I stop. I look over the locked square of railing and see two white bundles at the bottom of the stairwell.

I climb over and plant my feet on the small landing, hustle down the stairs to the space in front of the door, and pick up the bundle marked *R* for Raines. The other bundle is marked D. Denvie? If that's Randall's, we're in this together.

But where is everyone else?

I try the knob on the door next to me. It opens. There's

no one in the little room that's about the size of a large walk-in closet. It's empty except for a door that leads into the school and some stuff in the corner. Mops and brooms and buckets!

Did The Legend swipe them and blame me to see how I'd get out of it? Couldn't be. The Legend would not make me look like a thief. No. But . . .

I need to get out of here. Move away before someone sees me anywhere near this stuff. I slam the door, unload my syrup, shove my bundle into my backpack, and race up the stairs.

No one's here to catch me, but I jump onto my bike and race it to the other side of school before I deal with the bundle. I unroll what turns out to be a sheet with one rope attached to the top and another to the bottom. There are also two cans of spray paint—one black, one blue—and a blue envelope marked with an *R*. I open it.

1. *String the sheet up on the hooks that are already on the parking lot side of the school. Yours are marked with your initial.*
2. *Shake the can of paint before you use it.*
3. *Spray these words in black: The Legend Lives!*
4. *Spray over those letters in blue.*

5. *Take this note and the spray cans and throw*
   them in the garbage somewhere away from school.
6. *You have 10 minutes to do this and get out of here.*
7. *Come back downstairs at 2 P.M. Do not be late.*

It sounds wrong, but so did the flowers and the gum. I made those right. Besides, Matti and Kip know about this. They have my back.

And I have only ten minutes. I check my cell phone. It's one minute to seven.

I ride to the parking lot side of school. There's already one Legend Lives banner attached to the wall. Whose?

Doesn't matter. I find my R hooks and tie up one end of the sheet. Now for the other. My gut tells me to stop and look behind the other banner.

I was right. There's a smarter way.

I don't care what the instructions say. I take the sheet down and spread it on the grass. I'm not having my banner bleed through to the brick wall.

I shake the can. Stand on the side where the breeze is blowing away from me. And I spray. First with black, then with blue. I pull the sheet away and see remnants of my artwork on the grass. No harm. It'll grow, get cut, disappear.

I check the cell phone. I have only four minutes to string this up. I tie the upper left-hand corner. I tie the upper right. Lower right. Lower left. I go back to the grass, grab my paint cans and my backpack. And—

That's a car pulling up. A door slams. Now footsteps.

I duck behind the shed next to the loading dock, wait for the person to come around.

Someone to congratulate me?

No. It's Randall.

CHAPTER
▪30▪

He looks around then punches a number into his cell phone. "I'm here, Mom," he says. "No. I'm the first." He pauses. "No. You can go." Pause. "Yeah, I will. Bye."

I hear a car move around the front of school. He actually had his mom drop him off? He actually had to call her? Those aren't the actions of a true oaf. A true oaf would climb out of his bedroom window, stay in the shadows, and take pictures of me near mops and brooms and buckets. A true oaf would swipe my camera. A true oaf would bolt the moment after he threw Kip's cap out the window. Still, Randall almost killed Jackie Muggs in fourth grade.

I need to find out if he's really as he appears right now, looking as creeped out as I felt.

When Randall's down the stairs, I speed around the school to follow him from behind. I turn the corner in time to see him disappear to the parking lot side, then I move forward.

Even though he should be so wrapped up in what he needs to do and how fast he needs to do it, he's not deaf either. Halfway there I dump my bike so I can sneak up better.

I peek around the corner, and Randall's almost finished tying up his banner. His paint's gonna seep through the sheets.

I shouldn't care if he gets into trouble. He's done enough to make my life miserable. But if he messes up the school, things could get worse. For me. What if his paint is the straw that breaks The Legend's back, and they disband the thing just as I'm about to get in?

Besides, I owe him.

I hear Randall shaking the can. It's now or never. Now or never. Now or—

"Wait!" I come around the side of the building.

He puts on that face that comes before a fist. "What?"

I want to get the heck out of there, but I point to my banner. "I just did that one."

"Should I hold a parade in your honor?" He takes the lid off the can.

"I'm trying to stop you from making a mistake," I say. "Look behind both banners. Unless you want to mess up the bricks, you need to take the sheet down before you paint it."

He stares at me, stares at the banners. If he's Randall the oaf, he'll start painting. If he's Randall with the nice mom, he'll take it down.

He looks behind both sheets then stares at his. "The instructions say –"

"I know what the instructions say, and the banner police did not arrest me." I don't give him a chance to protest. I unloop the left side of the sheet. If he wants to slug me, let him.

He unloops his side, and together we take it to the back of the school to the same area of grass where I sprayed.

He stands, facing the wind. I should let him spray, but . . .

"Stand on this side."

He's still looking at me, all suspicious like.

Fine. "Unless you want the wind to blow the paint back at you."

He moves over, shakes the can again, and lets the black paint loose, writing the same words I did. He drops the black and shakes the blue. Looks up. "Why are you doing this?"

"I don't know."

"You don't know why you're making me spray sheets and steal soap and throw marbles in the gym which, thank goodness, got discovered before people got killed."

He thinks I'm the bad guy? "I'm not doing any of that," I say.

He sprays the blue paint. "Even if I believed you, which I don't, it's payback time."

"Payback for what?"

He keeps spraying. "For explaining the number sequence."

"That's what I am doing."

"Then move it. Grab a rope and hook it to the wall. You owe me."

He really thinks I'm the bad guy? He's delusional.

"Why should I help you anymore? How do I know you won't drag me into school and throw my head out the window like you threw Kip's cap? Or send me to the hospital like Jackie Muggs and hope no one ever hears from me again?" I brace myself for a pummeling.

But Randall's whole body slumps. "Are people always going to hate me for that?"

"You almost killed the kid," I practically yell.

He drops the side of his banner and stands there looking at his work. "Just forget it. Forget everything. Leave."

I should. So why do I feel like I'd feel if Matti slapped me or if Kip yelled at me?

I pick up one side of the banner near me. "C'mon. Let's finish this."

Within a minute we're done. No slugging. No dirty looks. No words.

There have to be more words. "Let's get out of here," I say. I pick up his cans, toss them into my backpack, then head toward my bike. I feel him follow me.

"Randall?" I say without turning around. "You didn't almost kill Jackie Muggs, did you?"

He's comes up next to me. "Why do you care?" He motors past me and keeps going.

"I get the feeling I don't know the whole story," I call.

He peers over his shoulder. "If you did, would it really matter?"

"It might."

He slows. Stops. Turns. "This better matter."

I nod and keep walking toward him. I'm starting to believe it might matter. Either that or I'm setting myself up for a punch to the gut.

He doesn't charge at me. Instead, he moves till he's up against the school. "My mom's all over what's our business and what's not, so you've gotta swear you won't say anything."

"Swear."

He looks all around. "Jackie was at my house and wanted to collect spiders to see if they'd eat each other." He stops, but I stay quiet and wait for him to start again.

"We found a bunch of them in the woodpile and put them in a pan, but they just crawled around and wouldn't fight. Jackie got so mad, he pulled out a cigarette lighter and torched them all, one by one." Randall runs his finger between the bricks.

I try not to picture the spiders going up in flames. My arm skin crawls. "Then what?"

"It scared me, so I went to tell my mom, but when I realized he was in my room alone, I ran upstairs. He had my hamster out of his cage and was tugging at it. 'Ever see a three-legged hamster?' he said. I lunged for the hamster. Jackie tried to dodge me, but he fell back and smashed his head on my dresser. He got a concussion and ten stitches, then his parents shipped him off to some school where he could get psychological help, which is the part my mom said should stay private."

"You should've said something," I say. "We were all scared of you after that."

"You didn't like me before that. You called me Tripper and Oaf and maybe I deserved it, but it's not my fault. When you get these growth spurts, well, none of you knows what it's like to wake up one morning all uncoordinated, with ape arms. Except Marco. Since he was bigger, he wasn't afraid, so I had someone to hang out with. And as long as he thought I almost killed Jackie, he didn't mess with me." Randall shrugs and looks away. "Well, mostly he hasn't."

"Mostly?"

Randall starts walking again. I stay right alongside him and wait for him to answer.

"For one," he finally says, "the cap."

"Kip's?"

"I just wanted to look at it. I swear. You saw my room. The Rams. They're It."

"Yeah? So?"

"I had the cap at the window, and Marco grabbed for it. He thought it'd be funny if he shredded it. I knew I could keep it away from him if I angled my arm out the window, arced it back over him, and tossed it to the other side of the room. Then I'd run to save it. Just when my arm was going up, he chopped at it and the cap flew up, and well . . ."

"That doesn't sound like Marco. He's been—"

Randall shuts me up with a look.

"So you don't like the guy. At least he stayed there after we ran out of markers. If you were so worried about the cap, why'd you abandon us? Why didn't you do anything?"

"I did," he says. "I found Mrs. Pinchon. Ask her. She said Mr. McKenzie would get out the extension ladder when he got back."

"He doesn't have a ladder that tall in his closet."

"I know," Randall says. He points to the shed. "It's in there."

"So, why didn't you stick up for yourself?"

"You wouldn't have believed me anyway."

"Yes, I—" That's not true. "No," I say, "not when I was stewing in detention."

"Sorry about that." He looks at me. "Hey, Trav," he says.

Only my friends call me Trav, but this doesn't bother me.

"You're still playing soccer next year, right? I mean, not football?"

"In case you haven't noticed, I'm not exactly built for football."

"Yeah, but I see the way you kick a soccer ball. Football always needs kickers."

"Don't know if I could live without soccer." I look up toward the stairwell, about half the school building ahead. "Randall," I say, "you know I wasn't the one who had you do the soap or the sign or the marbles. And I know you didn't make me do the gum or the syrup or the flowers."

"And both types of the blue envelopes?"

Both types of envelopes? I look around. No Matti. No Kip. They said they'd be here. They said they'd have my back. Instructions in non-shiny envelopes? Not from The Legend.

"Something's not right," I say. "C'mon!"

We start running.

CHAPTER
▪31▪

We speed the opposite way of the brooms and syrup and stuff, back toward the banners, around the corner and—

"Ahh!"

Straight into Mr. McKenzie. He *is* using me.

He grabs Randall's arm with one hand and mine with the other. "You!" he says to Randall. "And especially, you!" he yells at me.

"Ow!"

"Here I am, giving you the benefit of every doubt, and what do you do? You overflow my toilets. You steal my soap. You wad up my cafeteria with gum. Now this!" He throws our arms down and points to the banners.

I want to leave, but he'll tell Mrs. Pinchon, and I have no proof against him. So forget The Legend. Forget soccer camp. Forget soccer captain. And march me off to that school with Jackie Muggs.

"It wasn't us, Mr. McKenzie." But he can make it look that way.

"You say that every time. 'It wasn't me. It wasn't me,'" he says in a whiny voice. "Well, here you are. And here that is. And what am I supposed think?" He whips out a cell phone.

"Who are you calling?" Randall says, his voice almost shaking.

"The police."

"Wait," I say. "We didn't get the paint on the school. The person who sprayed that banner did but not us." I lift the edge of mine, then Randall's. "See. No paint." I run toward the grass. "C'mere. I saw what would happen if I painted it up there so we both sprayed ours on the grass."

"Is that your story, too, Travis's friend?"

"He's—" I almost say he's not my friend. "His name is Randall."

"Well, is it, Randall?"

"Yes, sir."

Mr. McKenzie stares. "How do I know you didn't paint the other one first? You could still be guilty."

"You have to believe us."

"If I do believe you about the paint, that still doesn't explain the other pranks."

"But I *can* explain," I say. "We thought it was—it was—well, it was the school telling us to do stuff. Not the toilets or the fire alarm. We didn't do those." I look around. I don't see anyone, but I lower my voice. "Today, though, things didn't add up, and we just realized it, and . . ."

This would be the perfect time to accuse him of doing all those pranks to get overtime pay. Except I know it's not true. Not the way he looks. Not the way he sounds. And especially not because he asked Randall's name. He'd need to know it to put the *D* for Denvie on Randall's bundle.

He glares at me. "And what?"

"And I really need to catch those bad guys. They're the ones getting me in trouble."

"So, there are bad guys now? And where are these bad guys? In your imagination?"

"They exist," I say, still keeping my voice down. "I swear."

Randall slips him the sheet of paper. "We have instructions."

"He's right," I say. "If we started this, why would we write instructions to ourselves?"

He reads them. "What's happening at two o'clock?"

"I don't know." I raise my head toward Mr. McKenzie's ear and whisper, "But supposedly they're watching us, probably from over there, behind the back bushes, so if you call the police now, we may never find out."

He shakes his head. "I want to believe you, Travis, but you're here with the evidence."

This could be suicide, but . . . "Do you have Mrs. Pinchon's number?"

"I do."

"Mrs. Pinchon?" Randall turns several shades of pale. "Why?"

"I want her to be here. I want her to see I'm not the one."

"I'm not the one either," Randall says.

I nod. "We're not the ones."

Mr. McKenzie leads us into the building so no one can overhear. He pushes some numbers into his phone and hands it to me.

The phone stops ringing. "Yes, Ralph?" comes the drawl at the other end.

"It's not Mr. McKenzie, Mrs. Pinchon. It's me. Travis Raines." I tell her the story of me and Randall being there. "I wanted you to know," I finish. "It was my idea to call because I want to help catch whoever's been making me look bad."

"I'll be there as fast as I can, Mr. Raines."

I press End, hand Mr. McKenzie his phone, and grow a way-too-big smile on my face.

"You want to let me in on whatever's so amusing, Travis?"

Why not? "I thought you were setting me up to get overtime pay."

His smile turns into a laugh. "No, buddy. That's not—"

Randall comes looming over us. "Um, Travis? I hate to break up this party," he says, "but we were supposed to get out of here after ten minutes."

He's right. "We need to leave, Mr. McKenzie," I say. "I promise we'll come right back, but if the bad guys are watching, we've gotta make this look good, like we got away with something."

He steps aside.

Randall and I burst out of school and keep moving.

"He forgot to check my backpack for cans!" I say loud enough for the back bushes to hear. We high-five. We laugh. We walk around to the front. He sits on the steps and calls his parents. I jump onto my bike, pedal down the main road, then stop on a side street, where I call mine. "Be home in about an hour."

It's 7:42. In just over six hours, I find out exactly who's been making my life miserable. First, though, I need to sneak back into school.

I weave around the neighborhood for a couple minutes and end at a street opposite Lauer. I chain my bike to the signpost. Look at the school. Coast is clear. Go! I race across the street. Aim for the parking lot. Jump behind the bushes near the door.

Finally Mrs. Pinchon's pickup pulls in. She walks toward the entrance where I'm sitting. I don't want to cause her a heart attack, so I rustle around. "It's me in here, Mrs. Pinchon," I half whisper. "Me, Travis. Behind the bushes."

She nods, unlocks the door, and goes in. The door shuts then stays open an inch from the doorstop she kicks into place.

I crawl into the school, close the door all the way, and hope none of the bad guys saw me.

When we get to her office, Mr. McKenzie and Randall

are already there. We give her every detail, and Randall's almost in tears when he admits he swiped the soap.

"And whoever you're looking for was here this morning," Mr. McKenzie says. "I checked the stairwell. The syrup and soap were moved to the space inside the door with the mops, brooms, and buckets."

"How's that possible, Ralph? It should have triggered the alarm."

He shakes his head. "The interior door trips the alarm. No one breached that. But they'll be back by two o'clock. And we know what they're planning to do with the syrup and soap."

"I figure they're not planning to make pancakes then clean up after themselves," I say.

Mr. McKenzie smiles. "When you get home, mix the two together and smear some on a plate. Let it dry for a couple days, then try to wash it off, but not under running water. We can't put the hall floors under running water. Try to wash it off with a rag."

I picture it. Sticky, soapy bubbles slopped all over. It'd take forever to wipe it up.

"Now," Mrs. Pinchon says, "back to the perpetrators. Do you know who they are?"

"I think it's Marco," Randall says.

"Marco Knox?" she says.

Randall nods. "He's been griping over The Legend getting all the attention and how someone should change that." Randall tells us things Marco's said recently, and it makes sense.

He started being nice right after I climbed on the roof. And he was there when I talked about the toilet paper. I want to punch him for using me.

"If that's everything, boys," Mrs. Pinchon says, "then go home. Do what you normally do on the weekend."

I shake my head.

"Now what, Mr. Raines?"

"We have to come back at two o'clock."

"Oh no," says Mrs. Pinchon. "We'll let the police handle it from here."

"You can't," I say. "If the police are waiting and we don't show up, the bad guys'll know we called them. And if it's Marco and his oafs, then either move me to east Micronesia or make a reservation in the nearest emergency room."

"Even if the police arrest them," says Randall, "it's not forever. They'll be back for us."

Mrs. Pinchon twirls her hypnotic necklace. "Let me get this straight. You both want to be here when the police show up so they can haul you to the station, too?"

"No." I tell her my plan.

"I can live with that," she says. "But if it's not working, we're stepping in."

I don't love that, but we agree.

"Now go," she says. "I'll see you both back here around noon."

"Two hours early?" I ask.

"Go home," she says. "You'll understand."

CHAPTER
▪32▪

My parents are relaxing with their coffee and the newspaper when I get back.

"How was your adventure?" my dad says.

"Not over."

"I had a feeling." He hands me a shiny blue envelope.

"Who gave you this?" I say.

"Some guy delivered it," says my dad. "And no, I didn't recognize him."

I race the envelope up to my room, unwind the string, dump out a seventh coin. Also a metal bar. It has a small knob on one side and seven round indentations on the other. I pull out the paper.

Seven puzzles solved.

Seven objects delivered.

Seven coins collected.

Now you'll find out why.

Be inside Room 117 at exactly 12:07 this afternoon.

Bring the bar and the coins. You'll know what to do

if you follow the rules.

Follow the rules? Hasn't that put me in a mess of trouble? It won't today. I know more.

And now I need my parents to know more, too. I go back downstairs. "You know this thing I've been doing?"

"Yes?" my parents say together like they've been rehearsing.

"There's this group of oafs—"

"Oafs?" says my mom.

"Bad guys who tricked a few of us—me and Randall and probably some third person—into believing that if we did what they said, we'd be part of The Legend."

"What we got wasn't real?"

"That part was real." And I explain the two sets of instructions and about the bubble gum, flowers, syrup, and spray paint. I dig into my pocket and pull out a business card. "Mrs. Pinchon's waiting for you to call so you know everything I do the rest of the day is legal."

My mom makes the call.

I pace around the kitchen and listen to a lot of "uh-huh"s and "I understand"s but nothing worth knowing.

My pacing expands to the whole house, and time drags more slowly than a sled with five hundred pounds of kids going uphill on unmown grass. If I would stop looking at the clock every two minutes, it might go faster, but what else am I supposed to do?

TV! I haven't really watched it since I've been off house arrest. I turn it on, but after ten minutes of barely watching, I turn it off. I go into the kitchen and manage to swallow a lemon-free, taste-free moon cookie my mom made last night. I head upstairs and zip the seven Legend coins and the metal bar into my knee side pocket. I take the pictures of Randall and the soap out of my desk and shred them. I'm done in here.

I go out and kick my soccer ball against the garage until my dad comes to kick it around with me. After a while he convinces me to get something to eat, so I have half a milk shake. Then he makes me wash up a little.

"It's just school," I say.

"But it's with people," he says. "And they have noses."

I change my shirt but not my pants. The coins and bar are already safe in this pocket.

Somehow the clock moves around to noon, and my mom drops me off at school. Mrs. Pinchon suggested I not take my bike.

There's a security guard stationed at a table inside the front door. Is he normally here on Saturday or special for today? I don't ask. He checks my name off a long list.

I doubt every person on the list is getting into The Legend. There are probably kids practicing for the play and the debate team and Science Olympiad, but I don't have the energy to worry about who else is here. I'm already worried enough about two o'clock. Also what to do with the coins and the bar.

I turn right and reach Room 117, Mrs. Bloom's science room. The window on the door is covered with a shade. Do I knock? Just go in? I crack open the door about an inch. It's mostly dark inside. "Hello?" Silent, too. I let the door close behind me.

I've been in this room every school day this year, and I cannot think of an obvious place for a bar and seven coins. I take inventory. Desks, lab tables, stools, sinks, closets, bookshelves, Bunsen burners, microscopes, ecosystem displays, static electricity maker, whiteboard, Whiskers, and worm farms. What am I missing?

Follow the rules and I'll know what to do, today's letter said. The rules! Why didn't I look at them when I was home? I can remember them. Keeping secrets. Solving everything alone and fast. Parents knowing. And the weird one. #6. Opportunity closing a window and opening a door. The window to the room was blocked off. . . .

So, what door's open? Lab table door? Closet door? Closet door! The Toxic Closet! That weird bar lock's hanging loose on the handle. The door is cracked open.

This has to be it. Either that or I'll be toxic in a minute. I wedge my fingers into the opening. Deeper and deeper. No alarms. No flashing lights. I pull.

No chemicals, either. Another door. This one has a weird bar lock, too, with its seven round indentations.

I unzip my pocket and pull out a coin. The nickel side fits perfectly into an indent. I grab another. Pop that in. Grab the bar. The bar! With seven circles, too. Dime-sized?

I put the dime side of one coin into the bar, and it clicks into place like there's a magnet. A strong magnet. I'm making a key!

I pop the other six coins into the bar. Fit the new key

into the bar lock. Grab the little knob on the other side. Pull back and . . .

Nothing. It doesn't move.

Shove it right. Nothing. Left. Nothing. Down. Nothing. Up. Something. Up and around? The bar lock rotates. The door opens. I put my new key into my pocket.

And I start down the blue-lit stairs.

CHAPTER
∎33∎

It would be a normal school staircase, going down one flight into the basement, but normal school staircases aren't behind Toxic Closet doors. And don't require keys. They do lead to halls like this one does. I follow the string of blue twinkle lights, which ends at another bar-locked door. I put my key in and rotate it up.

Standing on the other side of the door, with his or her back toward me, is someone in The Legend's blue robe. The person motions for me to walk ahead toward an open entry.

I take three steps and glance back and the person's walking the way I just came in, closing the door between us. I hear it lock.

I continue to a barely-lit room that is probably the half-sized, extra gym the school doesn't use anymore. I saw it on an old fire escape map. The room looks smaller than on the map, but it has a wood-slat gym floor and probably cinder block walls behind the blue curtains on the sides. A screen suspended from the ceiling shows clips of different Legend events, some from during my time at Lauer but most from before.

Mai Lin from my grade is in the first of seven chairs back here near the entry. In the second is Randall, an oafish grin on his face probably like mine. I take the third. No one tells us to be quiet, but it's like talking would break a magic spell. So we keep grinning and watching and waiting. Soon Sari Wolfe, the one who doesn't eew at worms, comes in. After her, one by one, three sixth graders fill the other chairs.

The video stops. Seven spotlights shine on the floor like an invitation to move forward. We do. Then, appearing from the two front corners, as if they've walked through the walls, blue-robed people parade in and stand before us.

Strrrick! A match lights a candle in the first person's hand, which lights another and another and . . .

I look around. Find the exits. See the fire alarm and extinguisher. Pay attention again.

By now all the candles are lit and illuminating the faces of The Legend members. First seven eighth graders. Then Natalie Levin. Then Matti and Kip.

The first eighth grader whispers, "One, two, three, four, five, six, seven."

They all nod and their voices whisper in unison, "It started with seven. Seven students. Seven pranks. Seven problems. Seven minds, looking for solutions. They found them, and in turn, they founded The Legend."

"The Legend." The voices echo and roll, the words repeating like a wave, one on top of the other.

"One, two, three, four, five, six, seven," comes the first hushed voice.

They file to the right, circle away from us, place their candles into holders, then return to the straight line, with seven of them holding up blue robes.

No one says anything, but it's like we're sucked into their ceremony and know to step forward, turn around, and let them help us into our robes. I zip mine up.

We stand there, still. The others circle around us, now with their hoods off, once, twice, and they keep going. And all I can wonder is why they picked me. I'm not possibly as smart as they are. But I am here. I'm here!

After seven circles they stop in front of us.

The first girl speaks. "You have solved the puzzles and followed that trail that's led you to perhaps the most secret middle school club ever established. The Legend."

Now the second girl. "You are all unique, yet you all possess each of our seven qualities: intelligence, creativity, kindness, ingenuity, leadership, spirit, and energy. You are made of the stuff of The Legend."

The third person, a boy. "The fact that you're here today proves you are worthy of reaching . . ."

Three words appear on the wall in front of us.

"The Seventh Level," say all the voices.

The symbol of The Legend, the square over the triangle, is now beamed onto the wall.

I grow this goofy smile. I'm here. At the end.

"The Seventh Level. Our highest level," says the next boy.

"Level One," the voices say in unison. "You are identified. Level Two: you are selected. Level Three: you choose to play. Level Four: you solve our problems. Level Five: you deliver what's asked of you. Level Six: you learn our secrets. Level Seven: you continue our tradition."

"If you are ready," says the fifth person in line, "please raise your right hand."

I raise my hand.

The sixth person, another girl, steps forward and refers to a book in her hand. "Do you solemnly promise to keep everything you say and do today a secret? That you speak only of The Legend with others who are members? That you speak with them only in a place you know is secure? That you welcome all future Legend members as we welcome you today? That you not reveal any fellow members as part of The Legend? That you contribute to the rich legacy of The Legend? And that you act honorably at all times whether you're representing The Legend or not?"

"I do," we all say.

"Welcome to the tradition of The Legend," says the last eighth grader. "And your traditions begins with another secret. Our secret code word, our password, a term you can use to alert us to situations that require our official attention."

They all whisper so softly I can't understand. Then they start turning up their volume, repeating the same word. "Lookout. Lookout. Lookout. Lookout! LOOKOUT!"

The spell is broken. The lights come up. The last eighth grader steps to the front of the room. "It's time to look out for our legendary adult leader and Legend member, Mrs. Bloom."

Dressed in a blue robe, she walks in from the right front corner. With the lights on I can see how The Legend members appeared. The wall in front of us stops just short of the walls on the side. I wonder what's behind the front one. I'll have to find out later.

Randall turns to me. "Mrs. Bloom was in The Legend?"

"Many of us are part of The Legend," she says. "Seventeen active members at this time of year. Ten when our eighth graders move to the high school." She pauses. "There's been a lot of magic today," she continues, "but it's time to break from the mystical for now."

Mrs. Bloom motions to The Legend symbol. "You'll count seven points to our symbol. Seven points you needed to fulfill. Seven puzzles to solve. Seven objects to collect."

To our right the wall curtain opens partway. Behind it are seven displays, mostly groups of pictures. I see my shirt button, my trash can, my nails, my doorknob, and my papers.

"These weren't random objects," Mrs. Bloom says. "They represent all the items we need to construct a wishing well, the centerpiece of the next school-wide Legend Event."

The curtain opens all the way to reveal a giant diagram

of a wishing well plus a full-size trash can, bucket, rope, bricks, pieces of wood, nails, and real supplies we'll use to build it.

"Our goal," she says, "is to find a way to grant three student wishes, randomly chosen. But more about that another time. We have other secrets to unveil first."

Mrs. Bloom nods toward the old members. An eighth grader hands each of us a booklet. On the front it says, *Lauer Middle School Handbook*. Pure genius. If someone drops one of these in the hallway, no kid will ever open it.

But I'm opening it now. It looks like school rules, but starting on page seven, there's a chunk of Legend information stuck right in the middle of other generic school stuff.

"You'll discover much of importance in here," Mrs. Bloom says. "Like how to access our semi-hidden page on our website. Who's found that?"

I raise my hand. So do Randall, Sari, and a sixth grader.

"Then the four of you know you need a username and a password to get beyond that. Your username is merely your last name but backward. Your password, you'll learn, is not in the handbook, but you will need the handbook to figure it out each time we change it. We'll explain how that works when your minds aren't so full from today. Temporarily use 'LoOkOuT,' alternating uppercase and lowercase."

Before that sinks in, she repeats what she said on money booth day. That the teachers aren't told anything about The Legend except on a need-to-know basis. Then she lets us in on so many more secrets, my head's about to spin off.

"I know you won't remember everything you've learned," Mrs. Bloom says.

"Thank goodness," I say.

She laughs. "That's why we have the book and website. For now, though, we celebrate."

I feel a hand grab my the sleeve. Matti drags me through the fake front corner of the room into a smaller room stocked with a huge cake, popcorn, candy, and enough sugar drinks to keep me wired for the rest of my life.

Kip comes over and we toast with 3 Musketeers bars. Then I go around the table and inhale a hunk of cake. I'm in The Legend! The Legend! And I can't stop the hooting inside my head until Randall comes up from behind.

He leans over. "I just wanted to ask if there's anything else you need to know."

"Huh?"

"From what I said earlier. The cap and Jackie Muggs? Is there anything else?"

"No," I say. "We're good."

"We're good?"

"Yeah. Except . . ." Why am I doing this? "You stare at us during lunch sometimes."

"Sorry."

"You can eat with us, you know."

He straightens up, a grin growing on his face. Then he goes to attack the cake.

Mrs. Pinchon has come in, and she witnessed that whole thing. She opens her brown eyes wide. "Things aren't always as they appear, are they?"

I smile. "Nope."

"Nope, indeed." Then she gets a serious look on her face. "Are you ready, Mr. Raines? Have you filled in your accomplices?"

"I'll do that now." I grab Matti and Kip.

"How'd Randall get in here?" Kip asks.

"I should've listened to my gut," says Matti. "I was right that day, wasn't I?"

"Yeah," I say. "And he'll be eating lunch with us from now on."

"Huh?" Kip's lips go pale.

"He's harmless. I'll explain later, but there's something else I have to explain now."

I wave Randall over.

"Randall already knows this," I say. "The four of us need to leave the party for a while."

"We can't," Kip says. "This is the biggest party you'll ever—"

"I know," I say. "And Mrs. Pinchon knows, too. Believe me. You will want to do this."

I explain the plan.

CHAPTER
■34■

To make this work, it can't look like we're conspiring. Mrs. Pinchon shows me all seven basement fire exits before she and Randall use two of them and Matti and Kip use another.

I go back through Mrs. Bloom's room and peek out the door. Down the hall Mr. McKenzie signals the all clear. I head his way, and he stays a distance in front of me to troubleshoot, just in case. But we believe all the fake Legend people will be waiting where Randall should be by now.

The clock in the hall shows 2:01. I stall for about five minutes then go to the meeting place, climb over the gate and down the stairs. I put on my swagger and pull open the door. Randall's there. So are Marco and five other oafs. They're all double my height and triple my weight, and if I mess up, I'm gonna be someone's snack.

"You're late," Marco says. He *is* the leader.

"Better late than caught."

He takes a step toward me. "What do you mean?"

"There were complications." I look at everyone there. "One of you was behind the back bushes this morning, watching. Who?"

"Doesn't matter," Marco says. "Why do you need to know?"

"Whoever was there saw Mr. McKenzie yelling at me and Randall."

"I saw part of it," says Karl. "So?"

"So after that I needed an alibi. I've been waiting for my guy, for fifteen minutes. He didn't show," I say. "But forget him. Why are we here?"

"Like I told the others," says Marco, "you're here because of The Legend."

Ha! But I need to let him play his game. I smile. Big. "We're The Legend?"

"Gotcha!" He slaps high fives all around. "We got all of you."

"So what are we? The anti-Legend?" I ask.

"I'm getting to that." Marco turns around. "It's time, Karl. Go!"

Karl runs up the stairs, then disappears from my sight.

"Here's the deal," says Marco. "The raw deal. The Legend rules everything, and it's not fair. We didn't elect them. They don't know what we want." His voice keeps getting louder. "And why is everything they do blue? They don't own blue. We proved that. We put our messages in blue envelopes. We pranked with blue paint. We'll show them. They're self-appointed suck-ups who wouldn't get into trouble to save their lives."

I try not to look at Randall.

"And they get all the credit. We can do legendary things, too." He high fives all around. "We started with bubble gum for sixth grade. Good going, Raines. Next week it's rubber frogs for seventh grade. And we'll all decide what's for eighth grade. All of us.

"Four of us started this, and we picked you because you have guts, you've been shoved around, and none of you will ever be part of the so-called Legend of Lauer."

I keep myself from laughing.

"And now that you're with us, you're in for life. You've already pranked, so if you back out, you're dead meat with the principals, the police, and with us. Together we will do things the school will never forget. Like what we're doing today."

I'm ready to get out of here. Put my plan into action. Know it's gonna work.

"Denvie, you got the liquid soap. Raines, you got the syrup. We poured them into the buckets Cranston got." He points to the gross mixture. "We'll slop it around with the mops and brooms. We also swiped graffiti markers." He pounds on the door that goes into the school, the one with the alarm. "When Karl comes around and opens up, we go inside and—"

"Tra-vis! Travis Raines!" Kip's right on cue. "Travis Raines!" His voice grows louder.

"He's not here!" Matti shouts. "Now we'll be late!"

"He's your alibi, Raines? That suck-up snitch?" Marco comes towering over me. "He's the reason I got detention last month. Why'd you think I tried to ax his hat?"

Marco's about to pummel me. And it looks like Karl, who just came in through the school-side door, is ready as his backup.

"He doesn't know why I'm here. I swear." I look Marco

in the eye. "I have to get rid of him before he starts poking around."

Marco's hand curls into a fist. "If you say anything . . ."

"I won't. And I'll take a witness." I turn. "Randall. C'mon."

"Yeah," says Marco. "You watch him, Randall."

I run up the stairs and jump over the gate before he changes his mind. Randall's right behind me. We jog toward Matti and Kip.

"Where were you?" says Matti. "And what's the oaf doing here?"

"He's good," I say. "He's our new friend. Take us as a package or forget it."

"Forget it!" Matti yells. "You don't control me. You don't say what I do or not do!"

I glare at Matti. She glares back at me. Inside I'm laughing. "Fine," I say. "Go with your little boyfriend, the two of you. Just give me my note first."

"I can't believe I'm doing this," says Kip. "You are such a jerk!" Poor Kip can't act to save his life. At least he's loud. He reaches into one pocket. Then frantically into all of them.

Randall gets up real close to him. "Give him his note."

Kip shrinks back. "I don't know where it is." He runs, searching the ground.

That was our only stall tactic. The police were supposed to be here by now.

Leave it to Matti to keep this act going. She pulls a pen and pad of paper from her purse. "Just write another one, Kip."

"C'mon!" I yell. "I don't have all day."

"Hurry!" I don't know if Randall's talking to Kip or urging the police to get here.

Kip takes the cap off the pen and opens the pad, stall-mode style. He writes and—

Finally! Flash of metal. The police stride from the parking lot.

I head-point in their direction. "Get out of here," I say to Matti, Kip, and Randall. I rush toward the stairwell, bug out my eyes, frantically wave my arms back and forth in warning. I mouth, *POLICE!* but even if those cruds can read my lips, they're toast.

I book it around the corner, into the side door where Randall's standing with Mrs. Pinchon. "Where are Matti and Kip?"

"I sent them back to the festivities," says Mrs. Pinchon.

I hand her my voice-activated tape recorder.

"I'm proud of you," she says. "And I'm sorry I ever doubted you."

"I guess you had reason."

A smile beams from her face but fades fast. "You do understand," she says, "those kids will implicate both of you, and I won't be able to ignore it. You weren't totally innocent."

Randall takes in a small gasp.

"He's not used to being in trouble," I say.

"I know," says Mrs. Pinchon. "So, Mr. Raines, Mr. Denvie. Appropriate punishment?"

I laugh.

Mrs. Pinchon's cell phone rings. She steps aside.

"We're in trouble, Travis," Randall whisper-yells. "You have to take this more seriously or you'll make it worse."

"It's okay," I say to him. "I know what I'm doing."

Mrs. Pinchon ends her call. "So, you were saying, Mr. Raines. Appropriate punishment?"

I smile. Big. "We'll be waiting outside our houses by seven o'clock Monday morning. You'll be our bus, our bicycle, and our legs for the week. And we get the honor and privilege of spending the mornings and afternoons in your office."

"Perfect."

Randall looks ill, but he'll get over it.

"It's not that bad, Randall. Really."

"And don't worry, Mr. Denvie," she says. "Your parents and coaches will know it's only for your protection. No permanent record."

He nods.

"And now," Mrs. Pinchon says, "they need you back downstairs. You're not finished."

CHAPTER
∎35∎

I don't get a chance to catch my breath. I don't get a chance to imagine what happened when the police charged in or when Mrs. Pinchon got there afterward.

"You think they really arrested them?" I ask Randall.

"I don't know, but if we get a whole week in Mrs. Pinchon's office, I hate to see what they get."

I don't hate to see. I'm excited to see.

"Hey, Trav?" Randall says. "Thank you."

"For what?"

"You didn't have to help me this morning or save me this afternoon."

I shrug. I guess I didn't.

We go back into Mrs. Bloom's room, through the Toxic Closet, and downstairs, where the other Legend members are playing video games and pinball and banging away on computers that were hidden by the other side curtain.

Mrs. Bloom waves us over. "I assume you've taken care of business?"

"Yes, we did."

She gathers everyone together. "As Legend members," she says, "you'll find you always need to be ready for the unexpected. The unexpected happened earlier this morning, but the situation is now under complete control, thanks to Randall and Travis."

People clap for us. Except for soccer, I don't think anyone's clapped for me before. Not when I truly deserved it. I try to stop smiling. I do stop myself from taking a bow.

"Thank you for your patience," Mrs. Bloom says.

The lights go down. The screen jumps to life and shows a person in a blue robe. He steps into the light and lowers his hood. It's Chase Maclin!

"Most of you know that I am an original Legend. Being a Legend not only helped give me the confidence to launch my career, it also taught me the importance of being an honorable person, doing my best, and giving back, even a little, to the people and communities that have given me so much.

"Past Legend members will tell you, my new partners, that I make every attempt to be there for this piece of your initiation. Today, however, it was impossible. I do promise I'll make it up to you soon." He winks. "See ya."

The screen goes blank.

"'See ya?' You think he really means it?" I say to Randall.

Matti leans over from behind. "Just wait."

For what? "Matti! Wait for what?"

Mrs. Bloom comes to the front of the room. "It's time to go," she says.

"Already?" My mouth can't help it.

"Already," she says. "But your day isn't over." She leads us through a side door, down one hall, then another. We climb a stairway to a storage room with desks and tables and chairs and boxes and an exit door. We're at the side loading dock.

There's a bus backed up to the edge, its rear doors split open, perpendicular to the school, butting the walls, and acting as a shield to the outside. No one can see us slide inside.

I recognize this! It's the same bus I rode in to deliver

school supplies in October. The one with the sofa-type seats and the dark glass. The one from Lookout Transportation Services. Lookout! The Legend!

I follow Matti and Kip and buckle up in one of the front sofa sections with the rest of the seventh and sixth graders. The eighth graders take the area in the rear.

The bus inches forward then stops. Mrs. Bloom and Mrs. Pinchon close the back doors.

"Everybody in?" calls the bus driver.

"Let's go," says Mrs. Bloom. She sits with the eighth graders.

Mrs. Pinchon sits with us.

I look at her. "Mrs. Pinchon?" I say.

"Yes, Mr. Raines?"

"With the bad guys? You really had my back today."

She nods. "I have always had your back, Travis. Believe it or not."

I mostly believe it, and I settle in, pretty much grinning. And I realize something. That really smart kid, Cambridge, isn't a Legend. Neither are some others I swear would be.

"Mrs. Pinchon?" I say. "How'd I get here?"

She laughs.

"I mean, lots of kids are smarter than me. Why me?"

"You have the seven qualities," she says. "You all do."

Now everyone is listening.

"You need to be smart to be part of The Legend, but it takes more than brains." She keeps explaining, but I'm not used to hearing so many good things from principals. That makes it hard to believe. So I quit paying attention. And while my mind's replaying the part when we busted Marco and the real oafs, she finishes talking, and everything's quiet again.

Shouldn't we be laughing? Shouting? Celebrating?

We're in The Legend! The Legend! All of us here! But where's here? And why hasn't anyone asked yet?

We stop at a red light.

"I need to ask a question," I say so everyone can hear. "Where are we going?"

"Finally!" The bus driver lifts his sunglasses. "It's about time one of you new people asked." As he turns toward me, his tiger chain whips around. "Has anyone told you I have a recording studio in town?" he says. "And have any of you sung background vocals on an album?" Chase Maclin winks before he drives on.

My mouth gapes open. "Are you kidding me?" I say to Matti over the cheers.

She shakes her head. Laughs. "This is real."

"Is it always like this?"

"You have no idea," she says. "There's always more."

More? I tighten my seat belt to keep from jumping through the roof.

I'm ready for more. Always.

• Acknowledgments •

This book has existed on a multitude of levels. In the first, when my author's learning curve was at its curviest, I was guided along by the people in my original online critique group, especially Lynn Fazenbaker, Cindy Lord, and Carol Norton, who continued to set me straight after we'd moved on.

In the book's second level, it took the wise and blunt advice of the YAckers—Diane Davis, Kay Frydenborg, Debby Garfinkle, Martha Peaslee Levine, Mary Beth Miller, and Kate Tuthill—to wake me, in the most pleasant and chocolatiest of ways, to some unpleasant realities.

Levels three, four, five, and six? I climbed those on the shoulders of my wonderful agent, Jennie Dunham, who rendered such verdicts as No and Not Yet and Still No until that day when she told me to sit down. "It's ready," she said.

And to reach its seventh level, I needed the eyes and minds and talents of the entire team at Greenwillow—Virginia Duncan, Steve Geck, Michelle Corpora, Sylvie Le Floc'h, Tim Smith, Patti Rosati, Emilie Ziemer, Laura Lutz, Barbara Trueson . . . and especially the editorial abilities and supreme patience of Martha Mihalick, who had to deal with my stubborn attempts to retain the unnecessary.

Each and every level has been heightened by the support of my family and friends (and occasional strangers), who have allowed my mind the freedom to break beyond its routine borders. More specifically, there's thanks to my dad's creativity in signing my birthday cards; to Cassie's unique way of asking questions; to Paige's unceasing readiness to help unpaint me out of corners; to one waiter's lack of attention in serving me mega-caffeinated tea; and to Dick, whose energy I borrowed for Travis long before I realized it.

And finally, thanks to you readers . . . and a word of advice. If your mother and your grandmother and whoever cooks among your circle of family and friends . . . if they make things you love, get the recipes. Today. So here's to some I got and some I never will. Here's to Grandma Josie's brisket, Aunt Molly's turkey, Debbie P's chicken wings, Donna's grilled veggies, Aunt Jeanne's brownies, my mom's everything . . . and especially to Bubby's moon cookies.